BEYOND REALITY

Dilvish, astride Black, the great metal horse, plunged into the fog as the land behind them exploded into a volcano of mud. They raced a hedge of flames along a boiling river. Inhuman screams rent the air, as fountains of blood gushed and tiny points of light rose from the dark waters amid showers of sparks. A winged, monkey-faced thing flew at them, shrieking, talons outstretched.

Black leaped as the ground split before them, revealing huge purple hands. Then Dilvish and Black entered a curtain of blue fires that turned their limbs cobalt colored and brittle. Finally they reached a saffron cloudbank and stopped, shuddering, within a protective circle Black raised.

The metal horse scarred the ground with a cloven hoof.

"So much for the easy part," he remarked.

THE
Changing
Land

Roger Zelazny

A Del Rey Book

BALLANTINE BOOKS • NEW YORK

A Del Rey Book
Published by Ballantine Books

Library of Congress Catalog Card Number: 80-68221

ISBN 0-345-25389-2

Manufactured in the United States of America

First Edition: April 1981

Cover art by Michael Herring

To Stephen Gregg,
Stuart David Schiff,
and Lin Carter,
who, in that order,
called Dilvish back
from the smoky lands;
and to the shade
of William Hope Hodgson,
who came along for the ride,
bringing friends.

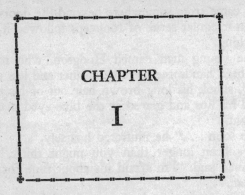

CHAPTER

I

THE seven men wore wrist manacles to which chains were attached. Each chain was affixed to a separate cleat within the sweating walls of the stone chamber. A single oil lamp burned weakly in a small niche to the right of the doorway in the far wall. Empty sets of chains and manacles hung here and there about the high walls. The floor was straw-covered and filthy, the odors strong. All of the men were bearded and ragged. Their pale faces were deeply lined. Their eyes were fixed upon the doorway.

Bright forms danced or darted in the air before them, passing through the solid walls, occasionally emerging elsewhere. Some of these were abstract, some resembled natural objects—flowers, snakes, birds, leaves—generally to the point of parody. A pale green whirlwind rose and died in the far left corner, shedding a horde of insects upon the floor. Immediately, a scrabbling began within the straw as small things rushed to consume them. A low laugh came from somewhere beyond the doorway, and an irregular series of footsteps followed it, approaching.

The young man named Hodgson, who might have been handsome were he cleaner and less emaciated, shook his long brown hair out of his eyes, licked his lips and glared at the blue-eyed man to his right.

"So soon . . ." he muttered hoarsely.

"It's been longer than you might think," the dark man said. "I'm afraid it's about time for one of them."

A fair young man farther to the right began to moan softly. Two of the others conversed in whispers.

A large, purple-gray, taloned hand appeared within the doorway, clutching at its right side. The footsteps paused, deep breathing ensued, followed by a rumbling chuckle. The still-fat, baldheaded man at Hodgson's left emitted a high-pitched shriek.

A large, shadowy form slid into the frame of the doorway, its eyes—the left one yellow, the right one red—taking light from the flickering lamp. The already chill air of the chamber grew even colder as it lurched forward, a hoof terminating its backward-jointed left leg, clicking upon the stone beneath the straw, the wide, webbed foot of its heavy, scaled right leg flopping as it advanced to enter. Swinging forward, its long, thickly muscled arms reached to the ground, talons raking along it. The gash in its near-triangular face widened into something that was almost a smile as it surveyed the prisoners, revealing a picket row of yellow teeth.

It moved to the center of the chamber and halted. A shower of flowers fell about it, and it brushed at them as if annoyed. It was completely hairless, its skin of a leathery texture with a sprinkling of scales in peculiar locations. It appeared to be without gender. Its tongue, which darted suddenly, was liver-colored and forked.

The chained men were silent now, and unnaturally still, as its mismatched eyes swept over them—once, again . . .

It moved then, with extreme rapidity. It bounded forward and its right arm shot out, seizing the fat man who had shrieked earlier.

A single jerk brought the man free of his chains and screaming horribly. Then the creature's mouth closed upon his neck and the outcry died with a gurgle. The man thrashed for several moments and went limp in its grasp.

It gurgled itself as it raised its head and licked its lips. Its eyes came to rest upon the place from which it had fetched its victim. Slowly then, it shifted its burden to a position beneath its left arm and reached forward with its right, retrieving an arm which still hung within a swinging manacle against the wall. It did not pay any heed to smaller remains upon the floor.

Turning, it shuffled back toward the doorway, gnawing upon the arm as it went. It seemed oblivious to the bright fish which appeared to swim through the air, and to the visions which opened and closed like sliding screens above, below and about it—walls of flame, stands of sharp-needled trees, torrents of muddy water, fields of melting snow . . .

The remaining prisoners listened to the stumping, flapping sounds of its retreat. Finally, Hodgson cleared his throat.

"Now, here is my plan . . ." he began.

Semirama crouched on the stone lip of the pit, leaning forward, hands resting upon its edge, the dozen golden bracelets on her pale arms gleaming in the faint light, her long black hair in perfect array. Her garment was yellow and scanty, the room warm and humid. A long series of chirping noises emerged from her puckered lips. At various points near and about the pit, the slaves leaned upon their shovels and held their breaths. Half a dozen paces behind her and several to the right, Baran of the Extra Hand stood—a tall, barrel-shaped man, thumbs hooked behind his sharp-studded belt, bearded head cocked to the side as if he half understood the meaning behind the sounds she made. His eyes were upon her half-exposed buttocks, however, as were a number of his thoughts.

A pity she is so necessary to the operation and cares not a whit for me, he mused. A pity I must treat her with respect and courtesy, rather than, say, insolence and rape. Working with her would be so much easier if she were, say, ugly. Still, the view is good, and perhaps one day . . .

She rocked back on her heels and ceased making the sounds which had filled the fetid chamber. Baran wrinkled his nose as a draft of air bore certain odors to it. They all waited.

Splashing sounds commenced deep within the pit, and an occasional thud caused the floor to vibrate. The slaves retreated to positions against the wall. Fiery flakes began to form and descend from somewhere beneath the ceiling. Brushing at her garment, Semirama trilled high notes. Immediately, the firefall ceased and something within the pit chirped in response. The room grew perceptibly cooler. Baran sighed.

"At last . . ." he breathed.

The sounds continued to emerge from the pit for a long while. Semirama stiffened, to begin a reply or an attempted interruption. It was as if she were ignored, however, for the other sounds continued, drowning out her own. The thrashing commenced again, and a tongue of flame rose above the pit, wavered, and fell, all in a matter of moments. A face—long, twisted, anguished—had appeared for an instant within the orange glow. She drew back from the pit. A sound like that of a great bell tolling filled the room. Suddenly, hundreds of live frogs were falling, leaping about them, tumbling into the pit, bounding up and down the high heaps of excrement at which the slaves had been laboring, escaping through the far archway. A cake of ice larger than two men crashed to the floor nearby.

Semirama rose slowly, stepped back a pace, and turned toward the slaves.

"Continue your work," she ordered.

The men hesitated. Baran rushed forward, seizing the nearest shoulder and thigh. He raised the man off his feet and thrust him forward, out over the edge, into the pit. The scream that followed was a brief one.

"Shovel that shit!" Baran cried.

The others hastened to return to work, digging rapidly at the reeking mounds, casting the material out over the edge of the dark hole.

Baran turned suddenly as Semirama's hand fell upon his arm.

"In the future, restrain yourself," she said. "Labor is dear."

He opened his mouth, closed it, nodded sharply. Even as she spoke, the heavier splashings subsided, the trilling ceased.

". . . On the other hand, he probably welcomed the diversion." A smile crossed her full lips. She released his biceps, smoothed her garment.

"What—what did he have to say—this time?"

"Come," she said.

They circled the pit, avoided the melting cake of ice, and passed through the archway into a long gallery with a low ceiling. She crossed it to a wide window, where she waited, regarding the morning's shining landscape through the haze. He followed her, stood beside her, hands clasped behind his back.

"Well?" he finally asked. "What had Tualua to say?"

She continued to study the flashing colors and the metamorphosing rocks beyond the streamers of fog. Then, "He is completely irrational," she said.

"Not angry?"

"Occasionally. It comes and goes. But it is not a thing in itself. It is part of the entire condition. His kind has always had a streak of madness."

"All these months, then—he has not really been seeking to punish us?"

She smiled.

"No more than usual," she said. "But the wards always took care of his normal hostility toward mankind."

"How did he manage to break them?"

"There is strength in madness, as well as completely original approaches to problems."

Baran began tapping his foot.

"You're our expert on the Elder Gods and their kin," he fiinally said. "How long is this thing going to last?"

She shook her head.

"There is no way to tell. It could be permanent. It could end right now—or anything in between."

"And there is nothing we can do to . . . expedite his recovery?"

"He may become aware of his own condition and propose a remedy. This sometimes happens."

"You had this problem with them in the old days?"

"Yes, and the procedure was the same. I have to talk with him regularly, try to reach his other self."

"In the meantime," Baran said, "he could kill us all at any time—without the wards, with his magic gone wild the way it is."

"Possibly. We must remain on guard."

Baran snorted.

"Guard? If he does move against us, there's nothing we can do—not even flee." He made a sweeping gesture at the scene beyond the window. "What could pass through that wasteland?"

"The prisoners did."

"That was earlier, when the effect wasn't so strong. Would you want to go out into that?"

"Only if there was no alternative," she replied.

"And the mirror—like most other magic—doesn't work properly now," he continued. "Even Jelerak can't reach us."

"He may have other problems at the moment. Who knows?"

Baran shrugged.

"Either way," he said, "the effect is the same. Nothing can get out or in."

"But I'll bet there are many trying to get in. This place must seem a real plum to any sorcerer on the outside."

"Well, it would be—if one could gain control. Of course, no one out there has any way of knowing what is wrong. It would be a gamble."

"But less of a gamble for those of us on the inside, eh?"

He licked his lips and turned to stare at her.

"I am not certain that I catch your meaning . . ."

Just then a slave came up from the stables,

passed by with a wheelbarrow filled with horse manure. Semirama waited till he was gone.

"I've watched you," she said. "I can read you, Baran. Do you really think you could hold this place against your master?"

"He's slipping, Semirama. He's already lost some of his power, and Tualua is another piece of it. I believe it could be done, though I couldn't do it alone. This is the most weakened he's been in ages."

She laughed.

"You speak of ages? You speak of his power? I walked this world when it was a far, far younger place. I reigned in the High Court of the West at Jandar. I knew Jelerak when he strove against a god. What are your few centuries, that you talk of the ages?"

"He was blasted and twisted by the god . . ."

"Yet he survived. No, reaching your dream would not be an easy task."

"I take it," he said, "that you are not interested. All right. Just remember that there is a big difference between a dream and an act. I have done nothing against him."

"I've no call to inform him of every idle word we pass," she said.

He sighed.

"Thank you for that," he replied. "But you were a queen. Have you no desire for such power again?"

"I grew weary of power. I am grateful just to be alive once more. I do owe him that."

"He only called you back because he needed one who could speak with Tualua."

"Whatever the reason . . ."

They stood for a moment, staring out the window. The fogs shifted and they had a glimpse of dark forms struggling upon a gleaming, sandy bed. Baran made a gesture near the right side of the window, and the image rushed toward them until it seemed but a few paces distant: two men and a pack horse were sinking into the ground.

"They keep coming," Baran observed. "The plum you mentioned . . . That's a sorcerer and his apprentice, I'll wager."

As they watched, a horde of red scorpions, each the size of a man's thumb, scuttled across the sand toward the struggling figures. Seeing them, the sinking man in the lead made a long, slow gesture. A circle of flames sprang up about the figures. The insects slowed, drew back, began to trace its perimeter.

"Yes. Now, that spell worked . . ." He nodded.

"Sometimes they do," she said. "Tualua's energies are moving in very erratic patterns."

After a time, the insects cast themselves forward into the flames, the bodies of those who perished providing bridges for their fellows. The sinking sorcerer gestured again, and a second circle of fire occurred within the first. Again the scorpions were baffled, but for a much briefer time than before. They repeated their assault on the fires and began crossing this barrier also. By then, more of them were moving across the sands to join the first wave. The sorcerer raised his hand once more and commenced another gesture. Flames bloomed in the beginnings of a third circle. At that moment, however, the drifting mists obscured the entire prospect once again.

"Damn!" Baran said. "Just when it was getting interesting. How many more circles do you think he'll raise?"

"Five," she replied. "That's about all he had room for."

"I'd have guessed four, but perhaps you're right. There was a little distortion."

A faint thumping, flapping sound arose somewhere in the distance.

"What was it like?" he said a little while later.

"What?"

"Being dead. Being summoned back after all this time. You never talk about it."

She averted her gaze.

"You think perhaps that I passed the time in some horrid hell? Or possibly in some place of delight? Or that it is all shadowy and dreamlike to me now? Or else that nothing intervened? An empty blackness?"

"All of these had occurred to me at one time or another. Which one was it?"

"Actually, none of them," she said. "I underwent a series of reincarnations—some of them very interesting, many quite tedious."

"Really?"

"Yes. In the past, I was a serving wench in a kingdom far to the east, where I soon came to be a secret favorite of the king's. When Jelerak reanimated my original dust and called my spirit back to it, that poor girl was left a gibbering idiot. At a most awkward moment, I might add—while enjoying the royal embrace." She paused a moment. Then, "He never noticed," she finished.

Baran moved so as to view her face. She was laughing.

"Bitch!" he said. "Always mocking. You never give a man a straight answer!"

"You've noticed. Yes. It pleases me to be perhaps the only person around with some knowledge of such a profound matter—and not to share it."

The irregular noises of approach had grown louder.

"Oh, look! It's cleared! He's drawing the sixth circle now!"

Baran chuckled.

"So he is. But he can barely move that hand. I don't know whether he'll get another one inscribed. It's even possible he'll go under before they get to him. He seems to be sinking faster now."

"Misted over again! We'll never know . . ."

The noises increased in tempo, and they turned in time to see a purple creature with mismatched eyes and legs scurry past them in the direction of the chamber they had quitted.

"Don't go in there!" she shouted in Mabrahoring. Then, "Baran! Stop it! I won't be responsible for the results if Tualua's disturbed by a demon! If this place comes unmoored—"

"Halt!" Baran cried, turning.

But the demon, a suspicious object held close to the source of its chuckle, scurried across a dung-heap and rushed toward the edge of the pit.

An instant later, the empty space directly before it seemed to come open with a sound like tearing fabric, revealing a brief field of absolute blackness. The slaves rushed away. The demon halted, cowered.

There was movement within the dark opening. An enormous pale hand emerged from it. The demon moved quickly then, to sidestep and retreat, but the hand was quicker. It shot forward and seized it by the neck, raising it above the floor. Then it moved, the dark area drifting with it, bearing its writhing, choking burden back over the heap, across the chamber, out the doorway and along the gallery.

It approached Baran and Semirama and dropped the creature at the former's feet. Then the Hand withdrew into the darkness, the tearing sound followed, and the air was still once more.

Semirama gasped. The object still clutched by

the writhing demon was a human leg, upon which it had been chewing.

"It's been among the prisoners again!" she cried. "I recognize that tattoo! It was Joab, the fat sorcerer from the East."

Baran kicked the cowering creature on the buttocks.

"Stay out of that chamber! Stay away from that pit!" he shouted in Mabrahoring, gesturing back up the hall. "If you go near that place again, the full wrath of the Hand will descend upon you!"

He kicked again, sending the large creature sprawling. It began to moan, it clutched the leg more closely.

"Do you understand?"

"Yes," it whimpered in the same tongue.

"Then remember my words—and get out of my sight!"

The demon rushed back in the direction from which it had originally come.

"But the prisoners—" Semirama put in again.

"What of them?" Baran asked.

"It shouldn't be allowed to regard them as its personal larder."

"Why not?"

"Jelerak will want all of them intact, to face his personal judgment."

"I doubt it. They're not that important. And for that matter, he'd be hard put to find a worse fate for them, on the edge of a moment."

"Still . . . they are technically his prisoners. Not ours."

Baran shrugged.

"I doubt we'll ever be called to task for it. If so, I take full responsibility." He paused. Then, "I'm not at all that certain he'll be coming back," he continued. Another pause. "Are you?"

She turned to regard the murky view beyond the window once again.

"I couldn't really say. And for that matter, I'm not sure that I'd care to if I could—at this point."

"Why is this point different from any other point?"

"It's too soon. He's been away longer than this on other occasions."

"We both know that something happened to him up in the Arctic."

"He's been through worse. I'm certain. I was there in the early days—remember?"

"And supposing he never returns?"

"It's an academic question unless Tualua comes around."

Baran's eyes flashed, then almost twinkled.

"Say your charge recovers tomorrow?"

"You can ask me then."

Baran snorted, turned on his heel, and stalked off in the same direction the demon had taken. As he did, Semirama counted slowly on her fingers until she reached six. Then she stopped. There were tears in her eyes.

It was moderately hilly country, with a rich growth of spring vegetation. Meliash sat upon a low hillock with his back to most of it, his arm-length ebony wand standing upright before him, its nether end driven a span into the ground. He stared past, to where the mists, pinked over with morning sunlight, shifted about the enchanted area, revealing the transformations and retransformations of the landscape. He was a broad-shouldered man with tawny hair. His mainly orange garments were surprisingly rich for the area and the situation he had assumed. A golden chain hung about his neck, supporting a bright blue stone which matched his eyes. At his back, both his servants moved about the camp, preparing the morning meal. He leaned forward slowly and placed his fingertips upon the wand. He continued to stare past it. As eddies occurred in the mist, as waves of shadows rolled, he turned his eyes to regard them. Finally, he grew still and assumed a listening attitude. Then he spoke softly and waited. He repeated his performance a number of times before he rose and walked back to his camp.

"Set an extra place for breakfast," he told the servants, "but put on enough food for several more people and keep it warm. It is going to be an interesting day."

The men grumbled, but one began removing vegetables from a sack and scraping them. He passed them to the other, who chopped them into the stewpot.

"A bit of meat there, too."

"Ay, Meliash. But we're getting low," said the older, a small man with a faded beard.

"Then one of you must do some hunting this afternoon."

"I've no liking for these woods," said the other, a thin, sharp-featured man with very dark eyes. "Could be some werebeast or other ill-gotten wight has wandered over."

"The woods are safe," Meliash replied.

The smaller man began dicing a piece of meat.

"How long until your guest arrives?" he asked.

Meliash shrugged and moved away, facing up the hill to the rear of the camp.

"I've no way of estimating how rapidly another will travel. I—"

Something moved, and he realized that it was a green boot beside the twisted tree ahead of him. A pair of them . . .

He halted and raised his head. A tall figure, the sun at its back . . .

"Good morning," he said, squinting and shading his eyes. "I am Meliash, Society warden for this sector—"

"I know," came the reply. "Good morning to you, Meliash."

The figure advanced, soundlessly. A slim woman, with pale hair and complexion, green eyes, delicate features, she wore a cloak, belt, and head-band to match her green boots; her breeches and blouse were black, her vest of brown leather. Heavy black gloves hung from her belt, along with a short sword and a long dagger. In her left hand was a light bow, unstrung, of a reddish wood Meliash did not recognize. He did recognize the heavy black ring with the green design on the second finger of that hand, however. Dispensing with the recognition sign of the Society, he fell to one knee, bowing.

"Lady of Marinta . . ." he said.

"Rise, Meliash," she replied. "I am here on the business you serve as witness. Call me Arlata."

"I would like to dissuade you—Arlata," he said, rising. "The risk is very great."

"So is the gain," she replied.

"Come and have breakfast with me," he said, "and I will tell you somewhat about it."

"I have already eaten," she answered, turning with him toward the camp, "but I will join you for the conversation."

She accompanied him to a trestle table south of the fire and seated herself on a bench at its side.

"Shall I serve you now?" asked the younger retainer.

"Would you care for some tea?" Meliash asked.

"Yes, I'll have that."

He nodded to the servant.

"Two teas."

They sat in silence while the beverage was prepared, poured, and placed before them, staring westward into the changing land with its mists. When she had tasted her tea, he raised his cup and sipped also.

"Good, on this cold morning."

"Good on any morning. It's a fine brew."

"Thank you. Why should you want to go to that place, lady?"

"Why should anyone? There is power there."

"Unless I have heard very wrongly, you are already possessed of considerable power, not to mention riches of the more mundane sort."

She smiled.

"I suppose that I am. But the power locked in that curious place is enormous. To gain control of that Old One . . . You may list me as an idealist, but there is so much good that it could accomplish. I could relieve many of the miseries of the world."

Meliash sighed.

"Why couldn't you be self-seeking like the others?" he asked. "You know that a part of my job here is to attempt to discourage these expeditions. Your motive makes it all the harder in your case."

"I know the Society's position. Jelerak may return at any time, you say, and the presence of intruders could create an incident involving the entire Society. You are an unimpeachable witness, as are the other four pointed about the place. To satisfy the Society requirement, I give my oath that I am acting solely on my own behalf in this enterprise. Is that sufficient?"

"Technically, yes. But that was not what I was aiming at. Even if you get through, the castle still has its defenses, and its master's agents are presumably still in command there. But putting all that aside for the moment, I strongly doubt that one of the Old Ones can long be coerced into doing good, should you succeed in gaining some measure of control over it. They're a rotten lot, and it's best to let them sleep. Return to the realms of Elfdom, lady. Work your charities along simpler lines. Even if you succeed, I say that you will fail."

"I've heard all this before," she stated, "and have given it much thought. Thank you for your consideration, but I am determined."

Meliash sipped his tea.

"I have tried," he finally said. "If anything happens to you within sight of here, I will attempt to rescue you. But I can promise nothing."

"I have asked nothing."

She finished her tea and rose.

"I will be going now."

Meliash stood. "Why hurry? The day is young. It will be warmer and brighter later—and mayhap another seeker will come along. A pair of you might stand a better chance—"

"No! I will not share whatever there is to be gained."

"As you would. Come, I will walk you to the perimeter."

They moved across the campsite to the place where the grasses began to fade. A few paces beyond, the foliage was bleached to a dead white.

"There you have it," he said, gesturing. "Approximately two leagues across, roughly circular. The castle's the highest point, somewhere near the middle. There are five Society representatives stationed about its periphery at almost equal distances from one another—to study the effect and to advise and witness. If you must use magic, you may find that your spells work perfectly well; then again, their efforts may be enhanced, diminished, canceled, or in some way distorted. You may be approached by creatures harmless or otherwise—or by the landscape itself. There is no way of telling in advance what your journey will be like. But I do not believe that too many have made it across. If some have, nothing appears to have been changed thereby."

"Which you attribute to defenders within?"

"It seems likely. The castle itself appears to be undamaged."

"Surely," she said, catching his eye, "one cannot base any conclusions on the condition of that castle. It is not like other structures."

"I have never known for certain, though there may be some truth in this. The Brotherhood—rather, the Society—is checking now."

"Well, I *do* know. I could have saved you the trouble. Would you know who was in charge of it when this thing happened?"

"Yes. The one called Baran of the Extra Hand. He'd been a Society member in good standing until some years ago, when he went over to Jelerak."

"I've heard of him. It seems he might be the sort who would have gone for the power himself if the opportunity were present."

"Perhaps he tried and this was the result. I don't know."

"I expect I will be finding out soon. Have you any advice?"

"Not too much, really. First, cover yourself with a general defensive spell—"

"That is already done."

"—and pay heed to the waves of disturbance as you go. They appear to sweep outward and around the place widdershins, building in force as they move. Depending upon their intensity, they may pass about it anywhere from one to three times. Their pace is normally about that of an ocean breaker on a pleasant day. In their wake, things are changed, and the effects on your spells will be most severe at their crests."

"Is there any period to them?"

"None that we have been able to detect. There may be long lulls, there may be several in rapid succession. They begin without warning."

He was silent then, and she looked at him. He looked away.

"Yes?" she asked.

"Should you be overcome," he said, "unable to retreat or advance—in short, should you fail in the crossing—it would be appreciated if you would attempt to use one of the means at the Society's disposal to communicate all of the particulars to me."

He glanced at the upright wand nearby.

"If I am dying and have yet the strength, you will have the record for the archives," she replied, "or for any other use to which it might be put—if the message can reach you."

"Thank you." He met her eyes. "I can only wish you good luck."

She turned her back upon the changing land and whistled three soft notes.

Meliash turned in time to see a white horse with a golden mane make its way out of the wood beyond the camp and move toward them, head high. He drew a breath at the beauty of the approaching animal.

When it had come to her, she held its head and spoke to it in Elvish. Then she mounted quickly, smoothly, and faced the changing land once again.

"The most recent wave was just before sunrise," he said, "and for some time, things have seemed clearest past those two orange pinnacles off to the right—you'll see them in a moment, I think."

They waited till a breeze stirred the fogs, and the twin stands of stone were momentarily visible.

"I'll try it," she said.

"Better you than many another."

She leaned and spoke softly. The horse flowed forward into the pale land. They grew dim and noiseless in a matter of moments.

Meliash turned back toward his camp, touching the dark wand as he passed it. He halted instantly, his brow furrowing, running his fingertips along its length, squatting beside it. Finally, he opened a soft leather pouch which hung from his belt, withdrew a small yellow crystal, raised it, and spoke a few words. The face of an older, bearded man appeared within its depths.

"Yes, Meliash?" The words came into his head.

"I'm getting peculiar vibrations," he stated. "Are you? Is another wave beginning over there?"

The older man shook his head.

"Nothing here yet. No."

"Thanks. I'll try Tarba."

The face faded as he spoke additional words, to be succeeded by that of a dark, turbaned man.

"How are things in your sector?" he asked him.

"Still," Tarba replied.

"Have you checked your wand recently?"

"I'm right beside it now. Nothing."

He communicated with the remaining wardens —an older, heavy-jowled man with bright blue eyes, and an intense young man with a deeply lined face. Their responses were the same as the others.

After he had restored the crystal to its bag, he stood for some time staring into the changing land, but no new wave rose. He touched the wand once again, to discover that the vibrations which had disturbed him had now subsided.

He returned to his camp and seated himself at the table, chin propped on his fist, eyes narrowed.

"Do you want your breakfast now?" the younger servant called.

"Let it cook. There's more to come," Meliash answered. "Bring me more tea, though."

Later, as he sat drinking, he spilled a little on the tabletop and began tracing designs with his fingers. The castle, so . . . A pentagram of watchers about it, thus . . . Waves spiraling outward in this manner, generally arising in the west . . .

A shadow fell across the diagram and he looked up. A dark-haired young man of medium stature, with dark eyes and a laughing twist to his lips, stood beside him. He wore a yellow tunic and black fur leggings; his link belt and the clasp of his brown cloak were of bronze. His beard was short and neatly trimmed. He nodded and smiled the moment that Meliash looked up.

"I'm sorry. I didn't hear you approach," Meliash said.

He looked at the servants, but their attention was elsewhere.

"Yet you knew of my coming?"

"In a general sort of way. My name is Meliash. I am the Society warden here."

"I know. I am Weleand of Murcave. I am come to cross the changing land and claim the Castle Timeless in its midst."

"Timeless . . . ?"

"A few of us know it by that name."

The Society sign passed between them.

"Sit down," Meliash said. "Join me for breakfast. Might as well start with a warm meal inside you."

"Thank you, no. I've already had one."

"A cup of tea?"

"I'd better not take the time. It is a long road I've chosen."

"I'm afraid there is not too much I can tell you about it."

"I know everything I need to know on that account," Weleand replied. "What I would like to know is how much traffic you have seen."

"You are the second today. I have been on duty here for two weeks. You are the twelfth to pass this way. I believe that makes thirty-two altogether, of whom we have record."

"Do you know whether any of them made it through?"

"I do not."

"Good."

"Small chance, I suppose, of my persuading you not to try it?"

"I imagine you are obligated to try talking everyone out of it. Have any heeded you?"

"No."

"There's your answer."

"You have obviously decided that the power to be gained is worth the risk. What would you do with it, though, if you obtained it?"

Weleand lowered his head. "Do?" he said. "I would right wrongs. I would go up and down in the world and to and fro in it, putting down injustices and rewarding virtues. I would use it to make this land a better place in which to live."

"And what would be your gain from this?"

"The satisfaction."

"Oh. Well, there is that, I suppose. Yes, of course. Sure you won't take some tea?"

"No. I'd best be moving on. I'd like to be across before nightfall."

"Good luck to you, then."

"Thank you. Oh, by the way—of the other thirty-one you mentioned, was one of them a big, green-booted fellow riding a metal horse?"

Meliash shook his head.

"No, no one such as that has passed this way. The only elfboots I saw were on a woman—not too long ago."

"And who might that have been?"

"Arlata of Marinta."

"Really? How interesting."

"Where did you say you are from?"

"Murcave."

"I'm afraid I don't know it."

"It is a minor shire, far to the east. I've done my small share in keeping it a happy place."

"So may it remain," said Meliash. "A metal horse, you say?"

"Yes."

"I've never seen such. You think he may come this way?"

"Anything is possible."

"What else about him is special?"

"I believe that he is one of our darker brothers in the Art. Should he succeed, there is no telling what mischief he may work."

"The Society will not take a position one way or another as to who may essay this thing."

"I know. Yet, one need not go out of one's way to help such a one with good directions and advice, if you catch my meaning."

"I believe that I do, Weleand."

". . . and his name is Dilvish."

"I will remember it."

Weleand smiled and reached out to retrieve an elaborately carved staff which was leaning against a tree. Meliash had not noticed it until that moment.

"I will be on my way now. Good day to you, warden."

"Have you no mount, no pack animal?"

The other shook his head.

"My needs are few."

"Then fare thee well, Weleand."

The other turned and walked off toward the changing land. He did not look back. After a time, Meliash rose and went to watch until the mists enfolded the man.

CHAPTER

II

HODGSON strained against the chains. They cut into his wrists, his ankles, but his weight loss during the month of his imprisonment gave him the slack he desired. With the big toe of his right foot, he continued the line he had been inscribing in the gritty floor, joining it at last with the one his nearest companion had drawn. Then he sagged and hung in his chains, breathing heavily.

Across the way, near to the entrance, Odil—who was shorter than the others—strove in a similar manner to draw a character into his section of the diagram.

"Hurry!" called the dark wizard, Derkon, who hung at Hodgson's right. "I believe one of them is on the way."

Two lesser mages chained to the same bench along the wall to the left nodded.

"Perhaps we'd best begin concealing it," one of them suggested. "Odil knows where his part goes."

"Yes," Hodgson answered, hauling himself upright again. "Hide the damned thing from the damned thing!" Extending his foot, he scuffed a clump of straw into the diagram's center. "But gently! Don't mar it!"

The others joined him in kicking wisps of the floor covering onto their sections. Odil completed another stroke at his character. The room took on an eerie blue glow, and a pale bird which had not been there earlier beat its way from corner to corner until it finally found the doorway and exited.

The glow subsided, Derkon muttered, Odil managed another mark.

"I believe I hear something," said the one on the left who was nearer to the door.

They all grew silent, listening. A faint clicking sound occurred outside the chamber.

"Odil," Hodgson said softly. "Please . . ."

The small man struggled once more. The others moved to conceal their pattern further. A wheezing sound reached them from without. Odil executed a pair of parallel lines, the second longer than the first, then carefully traced one perpendicular to the latter. He fell limp immediately upon its completion, his face glistening with perspiration.

"Done!" said Derkon. "If it, too, has not been denatured, that is."

"Do you feel up to it?" Hodgson asked him.

"It will be my first pleasure since I've come to this place," replied the other, and he began intoning certain preliminary words, softly.

But it was a long while before anything more occurred. They glanced repeatedly at the empty chains where the man Joab had hung, as the dark-streaked wall behind them. Derkon had completed the first stages of his work and there was a faraway look in his pale eyes, which stared straight ahead, unblinking. Hodgson had leaned toward him, occasionally muttering, as if attempting to transfer his own remaining energies to the man. Several of the others had assumed similar attitudes.

The creature appeared suddenly in the doorway and immediately sprang toward Hodgson, who was secured directly across the way from it. It was a red-bodied, thick-tailed, sharp-jointed streak, crowned with antlers, red eyes blazing, dark claws extended.

As it touched the middle of the concealed platform, it gave voice to an ear-piercing cry and pressed forward as against an invisible wall, the ivory pickets of its permanent grin clashing audibly upon its completion.

Derkon spoke a single word, firmly, without emotion.

The creature wailed and darkened. Its flesh began to shrivel, as if it were being burned by invisible flames. Grimacing horribly, it beat at itself. Then, suddenly, came a bright flash, and it was gone.

A collective sigh went up. Moments later, there were smiles.

"It worked . . ." someone breathed.

Derkon turned toward Hodgson and nodded, somehow making it seem a courtly bow.

"Not bad for a white magician. I didn't think it could really be managed."

"I wasn't too certain about it myself," Hodgson replied.

"Good show," said one of the two to his left.

"We've got us a working demon-trap," said the other.

"Now that we've insured our survival for a little longer," Hodgson said, "we've got to figure a way out of here and plan what to do once we're free."

"I'd just like to get out, call everything off and go home," said Vane, the nearer of the two on the bench. "I've tried both spells I know for getting rid of manacles, getting free of bondage, over and over again. Neither of them works here."

His companion, Galt, who sat to his left, nodded.

"I've been grinding away at the weakest link in my chain—the same as the rest of you, I guess—for weeks now, because nothing else works," Galt said. "I've made some progress, but it looks as if it will be weeks more before it yields. I take it no one knows a better way?"

"I don't," Odil answered.

"We seem to be restricted to physical methods," Derkon said. "We must all keep grinding until something better comes along. But say it does— or say we break free the hard way. What then? Hodgson has a good point. Shall we simply run for it? Or do we attempt to take over here?"

The sorcerer Lorman—the oldest—had hung silent for a long while, there in his shadowy corner. Now he finally spoke, and his voice was a croaking thing.

"Yes. We must attempt to free ourselves of these chains by physical means. The tides of Tualua make magic too uncertain. Still, we must continue to try the spells, for sometimes he rests and there are brief interludes when things may fall out right. It is our position that is bad in relation to his pit. His force goes forth in this direction before the swirling commences. There are places in this castle which are free of his interference—a long gallery near his pit, for instance."

"How do you know this?" Derkon asked.

"The force that blocks our magic has not interfered with my ability to sense things on other planes," the old man replied. "This much I have seen—and more."

"Then why did you not speak of it sooner?"

"What good would it have done us? I cannot predict when there will be an interruption in the flow, nor how long it will last."

"If you would tell us when an interruption occurs, we could at least try our spells," Hodgson said.

"And what then? I had felt we were doomed, anyway."

"You use the past tense," Derkon observed.

"Yes."

"Then you have seen something that gives you hope?"

"Possibly."

"Your vision is far better than ours, Lorman," Hodgson stated. "You will have to tell us about it."

The old sorcerer raised his head. His eyes were yellow and focused upon nothing present.

"There is a master spell—a great working, from long ago—that somehow seems to hold this place together—"

"Tualua's?" Vane inquired.

Lorman shook his head slowly.

"No. It is not of his doing. Mayhap Jelerak himself wrought it. I cannot say. I do not understand it. I simply feel its existence. It is very old, and it binds this place somehow."

"How can that help us, when you are not even certain of its function?"

"It does not matter whether we understand it. What would you do if your chains fell away this instant?"

"Go home," Vane answered.

"Walk out the gate? Hike back? How many guards, slaves, zombies, and demons inhabit this place? And say you succeed in bypassing them. Would you relish the walk through the changing land?"

"I made it through once," Vane said.

"You're weaker now."

"True. Forgive me. Continue. How can the master spell help us?"

"It cannot. But its absence may."

"Break a spell of which you're not certain—one that is sustaining things?" Derkon asked.

"Exactly."

"Granting that it can be done, it might destroy us all."

"It might not, too. Whereas if we do nothing, we are almost certainly lost."

"How would we go about it?" Hodgson asked. "One generally needs to know a spell's exact nature in order to unmake it."

"A simple but powerful channeling spell. If we got to the gallery and combined our efforts—"

"What exactly would we be channeling against it?" Hodgson asked.

"Why, the only thing in the neighborhood that flows with enormous force—the emanations of Tualua himself."

"Say we succeed," said Derkon, "and say that it does shatter the master spell—have you any notion at all what the result might be?"

"This place is known in ancient lore as the Castle Timeless," Lorman said. "No man knows its origin or its age. My suspicion is that it is a preserving spell. If it be broken, I feel the place could fall apart about us, possibly even fade to dust and gravel."

"And how would this help us?" Galt asked.

"There would no longer be a castle from which we must escape—only rubble and confusion. Tualua would absorb the actual backlash of the working, as it would be his force turned against the master spell. He may well be sufficiently debilitated by it to terminate the emanations. The changing land would be stabilized and our magic would work again. We depart, fit to deal with any normal challenge."

"Supposing," Hodgson asked, "that instead of stunning him, it whips Tualua into a frenzy? Supposing he lashes out at everything?"

Lorman smiled faintly, then shrugged.

"Six fewer sorcerers in the world," he said. "Of course it's a risk. But consider the alternative."

"You employ the singular," Derkon said. "There is more than one alternative."

"If you have a better plan, please instruct me."

"I have nothing better to offer, up to a point," Derkon stated. "If we were to free ourselves, I can see performing the channeling spell of which you spoke, to break the master spell. But say things fall out as you have supposed—we live through it and Tualua is incapacitated—I cannot see fleeing at that point. We would then occupy an enviable position—half a dozen sorcerers, united and in full possession of our powers, with an Elder One helpless at our feet. We would be fools if we did not move to bind him then, as each of us had originally planned to try. Our chances of success, in fact, would seem good."

Lorman chewed his mustache.

"Such a course of action had occurred to me also," he finally said, "and I can offer no rational objection. Yet—I have a feeling—a strong one—that the best thing we can do is get as far away from here as possible as soon as we can. I do not foresee the nature of the danger that will follow if we wait around, but I am certain it will be a grave one."

"But you admit that it is only a feeling, an apprehension—"

"A very strong one."

Derkon looked about at the others.

"How do you feel about it?" he asked them. "If we get that far, do we go for the prize, or do we run?"

Odil licked his lips.

"If we try that and fail," he said, "we're all dead —or worse."

"True," Derkon replied. "But we all faced what was basically the same decision, severally, when we considered coming here in the first place—and we all came. We will actually be in a stronger position my way—united."

"Yet, I had never realized the full magnitude of Tualua's strength until recently," Odil answered.

"Which increases the reward for success."

"True . . ."

He looked at Vane.

"It does seem worth trying," that one stated.

Galt nodded as he said it.

"Hodgson?"

Hodgson regarded each of them in turn, quickly, as if just becoming aware how important his choice would be. Derkon was an avowed disciple of the darkest phases of the Art. Lorman had been, but in his old age seemed occasionally to waver. The others were of the gray, uncommitted sort which made up the majority of practitioners. Only Hodgson had declared himself a follower of the white way.

"There is merit to your plan," he said to Derkon. "But say we succeed. Our ends will be different. We will all have different uses in mind, desire different employments of the power. The next struggle will be among ourselves."

Derkon smiled.

"Conflicts among any of us might occur in the normal courses of our affairs," he said. "In this, at least, we will have a chance to talk things over before doing anything rash."

"And we are bound to disagree on something sooner or later."

"Such is life," said Derkon, shrugging. "We can settle our differences as they arise."

"Which means that should we gain control, only one of us will be around long enough really to enjoy it."

"It need not necessarily follow . . ."

"But it will. You know it will."

"Well . . .What is to be done?"

"There are several very binding oaths which might protect us from one another," Hodgson said.

He saw Odil's face brighten as he spoke—also Vane's and Lorman's. Derkon bit back a beginning gibe as he noted these reactions.

"It would seem that it may be the only way to insure full cooperation," he said after a moment. "It will make life a little less interesting. But, on the other hand, it may well lengthen it." He laughed. "Very well. I'll go along with it, if the others will."

He saw Galt nodding.

"Let's get on with it, then," he said.

Semirama entered the Chamber of the Pit. The brown heaps were greatly diminished. The shovels were leaned against the nearest wall. The slaves had departed. Baran was in Jelerak's study, attempting to recover lost spells from moldering tomes.

Slowly, she moved to the edge of the pit. Below, the watery surface was still. Once more she looked around the room. Then she leaned forward and uttered a sharp, trilling note.

A tentative tentacle broke the murky surface. A moment later, her exotic speech was answered in the same fashion.

She laughed lightly and seated herself upon the edge of the pit, legs hanging over its side. She began a series of the chirping sounds, pausing occasionally to listen to more of the same. After a time, a long tentacle reared itself to rest lightly upon her leg, caressing, rising.

Arlata of Marinta guided her mount at a slow gait. Shortly after she had passed between the orange pinnacles, the wind had risen in intensity, periodically puffing gusts of extra force sufficient to whip her cloak into awkward positions about her face and restrict the movements of her arms. Finally, she tucked it partway behind her belt. She drew the cowl low, to shield her eyes, and tied it in place. The mists were swirled away about her, but the visibility worsened rather than improved, as large amounts of dust and sand became airborne. A brownish cast came over the land, and she took shelter in the lee of a low ridge of orange stone.

She brushed sand from her garments. Her mount snorted and pawed the ground. There came a series of delicate, tinkling sounds.

Looking down, she beheld a small shininess along the base of the stone. Puzzled, she dismounted and reached toward that portion of it that lay nearest her mount's hoof. She raised a broken flower of yellow glass and stared at it.

At that moment, a sound like laughter came out of the moaning of the wind. Lifting her eyes, Arlata beheld an enormous face formed out of a vortex of sand which had risen before her shelter. Its huge, hollow mouth was swirled in the form of a grin. Behind its eyeholes was a dark emptiness. Getting to her feet, she saw that from what might be called its chin to the place where its forehead merged with blowing dust, it was taller than she. The glass flower fell from her fingertips, shattering at her feet.

"What are you?" she asked.

As if in reply, the howling of the wind increased in volume, the eyes narrowed, and the mouth became a circle. The sounds now seemed to be funneled through it.

She wanted to cover her ears, but she restrained herself. The face began to drift toward her, and she saw through it. Something glistening lay uncovered in its wake. She invoked her protective spell and began one of banishment.

The face blew apart and there was only the wind.

Arlata mounted, then took a drink from the silver flask which hung at the right of the delicate green saddle. Moments later, she rode forward, passing the rib cage, right arm and head of a crystallized human skeleton which had been exposed by the eddying winds.

She rode on past the river of fire and halted again beside the iron wall.

"Dish it up," Meliash said. "I'm hungry."

He seated himself at the table and began recording the morning's occurrences in the journal he maintained. The sun was higher now, the day warmer. A pair of small brown birds was building a nest in the tree over his head. When the food arrived, he pushed the journal aside and began to eat.

He was into his second bowl when he felt the vibrations. Since these were not uncommon within the changing land, he did not even pause as he dipped the coarse bread into the gravy. It was not until the birds departed in nervous flight and the vibrations resolved into a series of regular sounds that he looked up, wiped his mustache, and sought their direction. The east . . . Too heavy for the hoofs of a horse, yet . . .

They *were* hoofbeats. He rose to his feet. The others had come silently upon his camp, but there was no stealth here. Whatever—whoever—it was, was crashing through the undergrowth now, moving like a juggernaut. No subtlety, no finesse . . .

He saw the dark form among the trees, only slowing now that it was almost upon his camp. Big. Very large for a horse . . .

He touched the stone upon his breast and took a step forward.

Abruptly, the dark form halted, still partly screened by the trees. Meliash began moving toward it through the sudden silence as he saw a single rider dismount a shadowy steed. Now the man was striding toward his camp, making no sound whatsoever . . .

Meliash halted and awaited his approach as the man emerged from the wood. He was taller than most, slim, light-haired; his boots and cloak were green. As he drew near, the man responded to the recognition sign with a version of the countergesture which had once been valid but was now several centuries out of date. Meliash recognized it for what it was only because history had long been one of his passions.

"I am Meliash," he said.

"And I am Dilvish. You are the Brotherhood's warden in this area?"

Meliash cocked an eyebrow and smiled.

"I know not from what place you might have come," he said, "but we have not been known by that name for some fifty or sixty years."

"Really?" said the other. "What are we now?"

"The Society."

"The Society?"

"Yes. The Circle of Sorceresses, Enchantresses, and Wizardresses raised a fuss, and finally got it changed to that. It's no longer considered good form to use the old designation."

"I'll remember that."

"Would you care to join me for something to eat?"

"Delighted," Dilvish said. "It's been a long journey."

"From where?" Meliash asked as they moved toward the camp and its table.

"Many places. Most recently, far in the North."

They seated themselves and were served shortly thereafter. Meliash fell to, as if he had not just eaten two bowls of the stew. Dilvish also applied himself with vigor to the fare.

"Your account, your garb, your appearance," said Meliash when he finally paused, "all speak of an Elvish origin. Yet there are none of your people in the North—that I know of."

"I have been doing a lot of traveling."

". . . and you decided to travel this way and try for the power."

"What power?"

Meliash set down his spoon and studied the other's face.

"You're not joking," he said a moment later.

"No."

Meliash furrowed his brow, scratched his temple.

"I'm afraid I do not entirely understand," he said. "Did you come here for purposes of journeying to the castle in the middle of the—" he gestured, "wasteland?"

"That's right," Dilvish said, breaking off another piece of bread.

Meliash leaned back.

"Do you know why I am here?"

"To help contain the spell that has produced the phenomenon, I'd guess," Dilvish answered. "To keep it from spreading."

"What makes you think it is a spell that has done that?"

Now the other looked puzzled. Finally, he shrugged.

"What else could it be?" he asked. "Jelerak was hurt earlier—in the North. He's come here to lick his wounds. He set that up to protect himself while he recovers. It may well be a self-perpetuating spell. The Brotherhood—pardon me, the Society—wants to prevent its running wild, should he expire within. And that's why you are here. That is my guess."

"It makes sense," Meliash replied. "But you are wrong. This place has indeed been one of his strongholds. Somewhere inside is one of the Old Ones—the ancient, tentacled kin of the Elder Gods —Tualua, by name. Long had Jelerak controlled this one, tapping its power for his own ends. We do not know whether Jelerak himself is in the place right now. What we do know is that Tualua has apparently gone mad—a condition not uncommon among his kind, if tradition speaks true—and that all of that—" He glanced toward the changing land. "—is his doing."

"How can you be so certain?"

"The Society was able to determine by specialized arcane means that the phenomenon you behold results from the emanations of a being magical in itself, rather than any particular spell. It is a rare thing to observe these days, which is why we have set up these stations."

"You are not here to keep it under control, should it reach out and become a danger beyond this region?"

"And that, too, of course."

"You are not here to use it as some sort of trap for Jelerak?"

Meliash reddened.

"The Society's position toward Jelerak has always been one of neutrality," he stated.

"Yet you barred his return to the Tower of Ice to keep Ridley in reserve against him."

Meliash frowned and studied Dilvish. Suddenly, then, his right hand dipped into a slit in his garment, emerging to cast a handful of golden dust toward Dilvish. Recognizing the material, Dilvish stood unmoving, smiling.

"You're that nervous, eh?" he remarked. "You see that I retain my form. I am what I appear to be—not Jelerak in disguise."

"Then how do you know of the doings at the Tower of Ice?"

"As I said, I was in the North recently."

"Those actions in the North," Meliash said, "were not Society-sanctioned. They were the work of a number of individual members acting on their own initiative. We are neutral on that matter also."

Dilvish laughed.

"Saving your commitments for the big ones?" he inquired.

"It is extremely difficult to get a group of temperamental individualists to take a position on any-

thing. You talk as if you were not yourself a
member. Speaking of which, you gave me an out-
of-date countersign—*very* out-of-date."

"I've been away for a long while. But I was once
a member of the Brotherhood in good standing,
albeit a lesser one."

"You continue to puzzle me. You want to ride
through a dangerous area toward a dangerous
place. Everyone else who has gone that way has
done it because he believes there may be a chance
of binding Tualua to his own ends—now that he
is not in full control of himself, now that Jelerak
is either absent or too weak to defend his own.
Control of that magical being would indeed bestow
a great power. Yet that is not what you are after?"

"No," Dilvish answered.

"That is a refreshing change, at any rate. Would
you be offended if I were to ask your objective?
I'm doing something in the manner of a survey—"

"I've come to kill Jelerak."

Meliash stared at him. "If you do not wish to
answer, of course I have no power to require—"
he began.

"I have answered," Dilvish said, rising. "If he
is in there, I'll face him. If he is not, I'll look for
clues as to his whereabouts and try again."

He turned back toward the wood.

"Thank you for the meal," he said.

He felt Meliash's hand upon his shoulder.

"I believe you," he heard him say. "But I am
not certain that you realize what you are facing.
Supposing you do make it through, and supposing
he should indeed be inside, or you run him to
ground elsewhere. Even weakened, he is the most
dangerous sorcerer in the world. He will blast
you, wither you, transform you, banish you. None
have ever faced his wrath and survived."

"I have faced his wrath. That is why I want him to face mine."

"I find that difficult to believe."

Dilvish shrugged off Meliash's hand.

"Believe what you would. I know what I am about."

"You think even Elvish magic would prove sufficient?"

"I may have something stronger."

"What?" asked Meliash, following him as he began to move away again.

"I've said all that I care to," Dilvish replied. "Thanks again for the refreshment. I will be going on now."

Meliash halted, watched him return to the wood. It seemed that a few words were spoken there—at first in Dilvish's voice. The reply that followed came in deeper tones. Then heavy footfalls moved off toward his left, and for a moment he saw the outline of a great black beast, Dilvish mounted upon it. In that moment, the light fell upon it in such a manner that it appeared to be made of metal. The hoofbeats became more rapid, circling the camp, heading west toward the changing land.

Meliash fumbled at the leathery pouch as he moved back toward the table. Seating himself, he withdrew the crystal and placed it before him upon the flattened pouch. He spoke softly, firmly. He waited, then repeated the words. After a pause, he commenced a third iteration.

The crystal cleared before he had finished, however, showing a long, thin face seined with wrinkles, tufted top and bottom with white, framing a black, shifty right eye beside a dead white one. This face was frowning. The lips moved. Meliash felt the word:

"Yes?"

"Did I disturb you, Rawk?"

"Indeed you did," said the other, glancing back over his shoulder. "What do you want?"

"Society business. This job I'm on . . ."

"It requires you consult the records?"

"I'm afraid so."

Rawk sighed.

"Okay. She'll keep. What do you need to know?"

Meliash raised his hands. He made a gesture.

"That was once a countersign to our recognition signal," he said.

"Things were a lot younger then," the other replied. "I remember . . ."

"If you can recall exactly when that one was in use, I would like you to search the archives for the membership records of that period. See if we had a brother named Dilvish. Elf. One of the lower circles, I'd guess. If so, did he tend toward either extreme? Also, is there reference to a metal horse or similar beast? I'd like to know anything at all that we have on him."

Rawk produced a quill, flourished it and jotted.

"All right. I'll do that and get back to you."

"Another thing."

"Yes?"

"While you're at it, see what we have on a current member—Weleand of Murcave."

Again the quill.

"I will do that. The first one sounds somehow familiar. I can't say why."

"Well, let me know."

"What is the situation there?"

"It seems unchanged."

"Good. It may settle itself."

"I've a feeling it won't."

"Good luck, then."

The crystal grew dark.

Meliash replaced it and went to regard the misted-over area which screened the castle. A lone rider on something heavy and black was moving away from him, fading.

CHAPTER

III

BLACK halted. Dilvish peered over the green scarf which muffled half his face, his right hand on the hilt of his larger blade, head turning.

"What's the matter?" he inquired.

"Not matter. Something less tangible," replied his mount.

"Is there something I should be doing about it?"

"Not really. I have detected a reality ripple—moving this way. All we need do is wait. It will pass shortly, missing us."

"What would happen if we did not wait?"

"You would be burned to ashes."

"We will wait. It is good that you have a feeling for these things."

"It may be somewhat less than perfect, however, in a place such as this. These are not ordinary spells, you know."

"Then Meliash was correct?"

"Yes. Those are the emanations of a magical being."

"It takes one to know one?"

"As they say . . ."

Dilvish felt a sudden blast of heat, and the landscape before him rippled and wavered. As this occurred, the wind died and the air grew clearer. Dilvish glimpsed shining spires, dark, moving forms, stripes of blue soil or rock, towering dust devils, fountains of blood—all far ahead, all for but a few moments—and could not tell whether they were mirage or substance. Then the wave passed. Winds dragging streamers of dust broke the prospect.

"Cling tightly now!" cried Black, and they moved forward at an incredible pace.

"Why the rush?" Dilvish shouted as they swept across the still-warm land, but his words were caught and carried away by the wind.

Their speed increased until Dilvish was forced to crouch low, squeezing his eyes tightly shut. The wind was now a single, immense roar all about him. After a time, it was like a silence, and in his mind he went back, back past his adventures since his return, beyond the hellfire, into the moist green land where the twilight fought the rainbow. He seemed to hear a voice singing, accompanied by one of the older instruments, an ancient song he had all but forgotten. The singer was a slim, fair woman with green eyes. There was a smell of wildflowers . . .

The sound of the wind broke in upon his reverie. They were slowing. He raised his head. After a moment, he opened his eyes.

They were moving upward, and Black's pace continued to decrease. Soon they came to a halt upon a hilltop beneath a brilliant sky. The wind was still. All about, below them, a fog drifted, churning in places. It was as if they stood upon an island in the midst of a foamy sea. Far off before them, the Castle Timeless stood, diminutive—a study in pink, lavender, gray, and shadow—in morning's oblique light.

"Why the speed?" Dilvish asked.

"There was more than one wave," Black replied. "I had to cross before the next one reached the area."

"Oh. Then we can rest here awhile and choose the best route."

"Not for too long. This hilltop is about to explode, becoming a mud volcano. But I have already determined the next leg of our journey, at least for a little distance. It seems it will be clearest if we bear to the right as we descend."

Dilvish became aware of vibrations beneath them.

"Perhaps we ought to be moving on."

"Behold the Castle Timeless," Black remarked, staring ahead.

Dilvish glanced forward once again.

"A place out of time," Black continued. "Long have I wished to view it."

The trembling of the ground became more pronounced.

"Uh . . . Black . . ."

"Built by the Elder Gods themselves, for some arcane purpose; destined, it is said, to circuit all of time; alterable, I have heard, but indestructible—"

"Black!"

"What?"

"Move!"

"Excuse me," he said. "I was transported. Esthetics."

Lowering his head, Black plunged down the hillside into the fog, his eyes glowing like coals. The ground was shaking steadily now, and in the portions of which he had view, Dilvish could see cracks appearing, widening. Wisps of smoke rose from several of these, moving to mingle with the fog. The winds rose again about them, though not as strongly as before.

Leaping among large, cube-shaped green rocks in a very unhorselike fashion, Black bore steadily to the right as the ground leveled and the fog was abated in patches. The sound of a terrific explosion reached them and splatters of hot mud rained nearby, though only a few fell upon them.

"In the future," Dilvish remarked, "I would prefer not cutting things quite that closely."

"Sorry," Black replied. "I was caught up in a beautiful moment."

He leaped a hedge of flames which sprang up before them, and for a time raced parallel to the course of a black and boiling river, down through a canyon where screams too high-pitched to be human filled the air. Along the river's bank, black flowers swayed, hissing and spitting. Tiny points of light rose above the dark waters and drifted off, to explode with soft popping noises, emitting noxious odors amid showers of sparks. The ground continued to shake and the dark waters overleaped their banks in places, staining the rocks and the land about with tarlike films. A winged, monkey-faced thing the size of a large bird flew at them, shrieking, talons outstretched. Dilvish cut at it several times, but it eluded his blade. Finally, it passed too near Black's head. He breathed a flame upon it and it fell to the ground to be stepped on.

The river vanished into a steaming cavern, wails echoing within it. The ground split before them and Black leaped the chasm. It closed behind them with a grinding sound, and rocks and sand were shaken down upon them from a height to the left.

The far mouth of the canyon was hung with a screen of blue fires. Dilvish drew his cloak more tightly about him and Black increased his pace. As they rushed through, Dilvish shuddered at an intense cold, rather than the heat he had expected. Looking down, he discovered that both he and Black had become a rich cobalt color. His limbs felt stiff, almost brittle.

"It will pass! It will pass in moments!" Black cried.

It did pass, somewhere within a yellow cloudbank, but this took longer than a few moments. They stood shuddering within a protective circle Black had raised, and the color and stiffness were slowly leached away. The winds were minimal here. Dilvish exercised his fingers and massaged his hands and biceps.

"So much for the easy part," Black remarked after a time.

"I hope that you are joking."

Black scarred the ground with a cloven hoof.

"No," he answered. "I am afraid that the emanations are stronger closer to the center of things."

"Have you any special plan of attack for that area?"

"Every protective spell I know is upon us," he said, "but that can only be one line of defense. Tualua, who dreams and hurts within, is so much stronger than I am that any direct encounter could overwhelm them. I must count on my perceptions, my speed, and our combined strength and ingenuity."

"I was afraid that was the case."

"They have served us well thus far."

"Then why are we moving—circle and all?"

"We are not moving."

"I think we are."

Black raised his head and stared through the fogs. The ground beneath them seemed firm enough now, but . . .

"Something does seem to be happening," he finally admitted. "The farthest rock I can see appears to be changing its position. I am going to risk a small spell. It may achieve nothing, it may rebound upon us, its effect may be distorted. But I would like to stir up the wind to clear the prospect —long enough to view our situation in better perspective."

"Go ahead."

Dilvish braced himself and waited. Black muttered in Mabrahoring. The errant gush which had been buffeting them settled, took on a uniform direction for a few moments, then shifted. It was several minutes after that that a steady wind came at them from the right. Black had grown silent by then, and both of them remained motionless, staring ahead.

Gradually, the fog bank began a leftward movement. A faint, lightninglike flicker occurred within it. It began to grow thin in patches, but the drifting vapors filled these areas almost immediately.

Then, as they watched, it all seemed to break loose and race away, revealing a dark prospect under sunny skies . . .

They were moving. Everything seemed to be moving in relation to the distant castle itself, which stood revealed again, salmon pink and orange. Only some things were moving faster than others . . .

They were drifting toward their right. The features of the landscape immediately before them also seemed to be drifting toward the right, and those more distant appeared to be moving faster. At a greater distance, however, bright rocks and sparkling glassy trees were racing leftward.

"I don't understand . . ." Black began.

The land had acquired ripples. The area where they rested, which had been low, was now rising. Dilvish, at a higher eye level than Black, was first to see and understand.

"Gods!" he exclaimed.

Far below and ahead was an enormous circular opening in a depressed area. The landscape was winding itself about it, spiraling inward; possessed of an abnormal plasticity, rocks and shrubs, logs and litter were all drawn toward that great dark hole and swirled about it, to vanish over its edges, along with the entire surface layer of soil upon which they rested.

"It's like a whirlpool . . ." Dilvish said, turning his head to look behind him.

In that distance also, things were moving in the opposite direction. Only . . .

"At least we are nearer the outer edge than the center," he said. "We had better get away quickly, though."

Black reared and remained upright for long seconds. Then he dropped heavily to the ground and turned to face the north. He began to move, breaking the circle which guarded them.

"This may work to our advantage," he offered. "We are being borne westward as we head toward the turning edge. By the time we depart the disturbed area, it will have carried us nearer to our goal."

He increased his pace.

"It sounds good," said Dilvish, "but I wonder . . . ?"

"What?"

"When we get to the edge—the place where this land platform ends and the stable ground begins . . ."

"Yes. I see what you mean."

Black moved even faster.

"That dark, curving line farther ahead . . ." Black said as he half rose again. "The ground does seem to be in turmoil there."

They raced on toward the dark band. Stray wisps of fog were blown past them. A low, growling sound now reached their ears.

"It does seem fairly wide."

"Yes."

The vibrations came to them. Ahead, a river of grinding rocks and soil seethed, crunching, like a boiling moat. As they drew nearer, the sounds grew louder. The ground began to dip and rock beneath Black's hoofs, and he slowed, finally halting perhaps fifteen paces from the place where the turmoil began.

Dilvish dismounted and moved slowly forward. A sudden dropping and recovery of the land threw him to one side, but his elfbooted feet moved with uncanny precision to preserve his balance. A log flashed by within the area of turbulence, moving as though it rode atop a horizontal avalanche. It struck a slower-moving stone with a dull sound, upended, and was ground to splinters before his eyes. Stooping, Dilvish seized a head-sized stone and raised it to shoulder level. This he cast out before him. It skipped several times before it was borne away atop the rush to his right. Dilvish stood waiting for a time, adjusting his footing in response to the landswells; then he took hold of another stone and repeated the performance, with the same results. He took a step forward. Several larger stones passed. He looked up and to his left, to where the castle seemed to be inching from left to right along the horizon. He took two more steps, then halted again.

"You might be able to," Black called, "if you time it just right. I'll keep watch for the proper steppingstones and call out to you. The elfboots should carry you."

Dilvish shook his head and turned back.

"No," he said, mounting again. "We have to go together."

"It is too far for me to leap."

"Then we wait until something large comes along."

"Risky. But it would seem to be the only way. All right."

Black reared again and peered upstream.

"Nothing suitable in sight."

He turned on his hind legs until he was facing back in the direction from which he had come.

"I can see the area we left. It's a lot nearer the hole."

"I can see a big rock coming."

Black turned and dropped almost immediately. The castle was now directly ahead and drifting to the right.

"Hold very tightly," Black said. "If I fall, try to spring from my body and keep going."

Black moved into a new position facing the dark and grumbling river of debris. The ground beneath them was raised, lowered, raised again. Dilvish leaned forward and squeezed until his legs ached. He turned his head to the left. He heard a distant booming sound, almost like a giant's laugh. He saw a sheet of flame fall from the heavens, disappearing at some point far ahead. Castle Timeless glistened like an amethyst now. The ground rocked gently, and there came a sound as of a massive gong being repeatedly struck, followed by a shattering noise, as if an entire wall of windows had suddenly given way somewhere. The dark river continued its crashing, its rumbling.

"Here it comes," Black announced.

Dilvish saw the half-submerged boulder again, rounding the bend with some difficulty, pushing toward them . . .

He tried to judge its pace. He closed his eyes and opened them again. A streamer of fog wound its way past.

"Now!" Black cried.

Suddenly they were moving. Dilvish thought it was too soon. The rock appeared as if it were caught for a moment and sinking further. Its surface seemed to offer no purchase for even the most careful feet . . .

They were in the air.

Involuntarily, Dilvish closed his eyes again. His teeth were jolted by the force of the contact. Black's body twisted beneath him, and he thought that they were slipping, falling.

He opened his eyes to find them rising through the air once again. He clenched his jaw.

They struck solid ground and kept moving. Dilvish straightened and exhaled, realizing he had been holding his breath. They were southwest of the castle and racing across a rocky plain, among fuming holes.

Black paused for a moment when they had mounted a pebbly hillock and looked back.

"Not bad," he said. "I wasn't sure."

Then he started down the farther slopes, bearing to the right.

"I wonder where it all goes," Dilvish said.

"What?"

"The stuff being drawn into that hole."

"I believe it will be spit out again somewhere

else," said Black, increasing his pace as they approached a sandy field.

"Comforting thought."

There came a rustling sound as they struck the sandy stretch. Small, dark, moving things began to appear below, Dilvish noted almost subliminally, growing like rapid weeds about them. The sand was then disturbed before them, and larger, faster versions of the same broke the surface, wriggling upward.

"Fingers!" Dilvish exclaimed, almost to himself.

Black did not reply, but raced on as large purple hands came up to clutch at them, waving and grasping, higher now. He trod upon them and his metal limbs tore free of them. Ahead, they rose to even greater heights, long, hairy arms like stalks in their way. Dilvish felt something brush against his right foot, and his blade came into his hand. He began swinging it downward, lopping grasping fingers which came too near. Black lowered his head and breathed flames to scorch the ground before him.

Mist rose in depressed areas about them, but this stayed at ground level, the air itself remaining clear beneath a bright blue sky with but a few puffs of cloud to the west. The castle, only slightly nearer now, glittered as if fire from the sunlight reflected upon its many panes of glass.

Dilvish began to perspire as he swung his blade on both sides at the hands, which continued to rise in profusion. They neared the far end of the field, where the land dropped downward out of sight beyond a low, dunelike ridge. As they approached it, the ground heaved and the most massive hand yet began to work its way free of the earth. Dilvish felt Black's strides lengthening, and bones crunched and snapped beneath them as they almost flew the final distance. Black's head was raised and his fires had been remitted. The palm of his huge hand was rising directly in their path.

Dilvish knew what was about to follow even before they left the ground, arcing through the air. The hand was reaching, still rising, as Black sprang. Dilvish struck outward and down at the nearest finger, feeling his blade strike and cut deeply. The hand suddenly clenched into a tight fist, completely clearing their way. A bleeding log of a finger struck the ground and rolled back down the dune.

Then they were descending. The slope was steeper than anticipated, but it was its hard, sleek, shiny quality which caused Dilvish to stiffen the moment before Black's hoofs struck. It was a side of a large, bowl-shaped depression, at the bottom of which lay a still, steaming pool. Sulfurous fumes filled the air here, and something suspiciously like a partly decomposed human torso floated in the yellow waters, along with smaller, possibly once-living objects.

As they struck the glistening surface, Black's hoofs immediately went out from under him and he toppled to the left. Dilvish sprang free so as not to be crushed, casting himself backward and to the side, rolling, blade still in hand.

The elfboots touched the surface and held. Dilvish threw his left arm crossbody and rolled to his right, catching hold of Black's right flank. As Black continued to slide, Dilvish's shinbones felt as if they were about to snap as the elfboots maintained their purchase. He shuffled his feet, breaking the contact, sheathed his blade, rolled onto his stomach and caught hold of Black with both hands, to be dragged forward, sprawled behind his mount.

He moved his feet again, gaining traction, rose

into a crouched position, still holding on to Black. In the meantime, Black's front hoofs continued to flail, striking deep gouges as he slid head-foremost toward the pool.

Dilvish began moving his grip, one hand at a time, working his way forward along Black's left side, his back, until he caught hold of his neck. He moved until he was in advance of his sliding mount, the elfboots locking with each step as he began pushing upward. His shoulders and thighs strained, his joints creaked, but Black began slowing and the movements of his forelimbs became more deliberate, the force of each thrust better directed.

The smell of the pool grew heavier, irritating his nostrils; and looking past Black, Dilvish could see that they had descended a major portion of the slope. He did not look behind him, but redoubled his efforts at stabilization.

Black's right forefoot struck and held, scoring the slick surface deeply, sending up a great shower of glassy particles. Then his left foot caught and Dilvish heaved with all of his strength. Black rose on both legs, his hindquarters still depressed, legs shuffling, digging. Dilvish caught hold of him about the neck and locked his legs, straining forward, upward.

Black halted, reared his hindquarters, stood immobile. Dilvish relaxed gradually, took a deep breath, began coughing as the noxious fumes entered his lungs.

"Don't," said Black, "take even another step backward."

Dilvish looked behind him.

The scummy waters lapped gently at a place less than a pace away. Dilvish shuddered. Looking further, he saw that it was indeed the remains of a human body drifting near the pool's center, bones exposed in places. The water was darker about it. He could almost see the decomposition continuing. He looked away.

"What now?" Black asked. "I know of no spell sufficiently specialized to cover situations such as this."

Dilvish smiled faintly and looked back up along the way they had descended.

"Offhand, I'd say we must do it the hard way," he remarked. "Let me test this slick stuff."

He removed his hand slowly from Black's neck, straightened and drew his blade. He took several paces to his left, raised the weapon, and brought it crashing down upon the smooth, sloping surface. The blade smashed its way through several inches of the material, and fracture lines spread about it for a full handspan in every direction.

"It can be done," Dilvish announced. "If I chop a series of holds along here, we can get you turned around and headed back up."

"Do that," said Black, "and I'll be able to make my own holds going up. I feel rather delicately poised at the moment, though."

"Yes," said Dilvish, coughing. "Don't do anything that requires movement."

He turned and assailed the slope once again. Chips flew.

After several minutes, he had hacked out a set of parallel tracks over eight feet in length, heading off to Black's right.

"How does that look?" he asked.

"Once I'm onto them, I'll feel uplifted in spirit as well as in body," Black replied. "Then I suppose it will be best to proceed in a straight line, right on up that side."

"I'd think it would," Dilvish said, sheathing his blade and moving back to a position to the left of

Black's head. "I'm going to be pushing up against you as you move across. Right foot first, I'd say." He took hold and braced his shoulder against Black's neck. "Any time you're ready."

Gingerly, Black raised his right forefoot and extended it, turning his body slowly. He placed the foot upon the far track, then shifted his weight further in that direction.

"The next one should be the real test."

He raised his left forefoot. Immediately, Dilvish felt increased pressure. He strained upward as Black moved the foot. His breath burned in his nostrils. Slowly, the foot came to rest upon the nearer track. The weight did not lift, however. Black was now moving his left hind leg into the niche just vacated. When he had achieved this, he brought the right hind leg forward.

"Two more steps . . ." he said softly, then quickly transferred the right hind leg to the farther track.

"Now . . ."

Dilvish continued the pressure as Black slid by, moving the first leg up to the track. Then he took several steps forward and Dilvish sighed, coughed, and stretched.

"Fine," Black said. "Fine."

Dilvish tied his scarf about his nose and mouth, then moved up beside Black once again, remaining between him and the pool. Black proceeded to the ends of the tracks.

"Now what?" Dilvish asked.

"No problem. Watch."

Black's right forefoot flashed forward, smashing a large hole within the glossy surface. It remained there as his left struck another, higher. He drew himself up and the right moved again. Soon his hind feet were moving into the spaces vacated.

"By the way, thanks," he said, driving another cloven hoof forward.

Dilvish rested his right hand upon Black's back and matched his slow pace.

"The sky seems to have darkened during our sojourn below," he observed.

"The emanations are very strong," Black said. "But I do not feel any change waves moving this way."

"What does that mean?"

"Almost anything."

The sky continued to darken to an almost twilit depth as they made their way upward. After several minutes they heard a short, sharp shriek from above, and a dark form slid over the rim, high to their left.

"It's a man!" Black cried.

Dilvish's hands flew to his waist as he moved to the left and called out: "Here!"

His belt came free in his hands and he cast it out before him, the weight of the heavy buckle bearing it directly into the sliding man's path. A long stick came bouncing past, almost striking Dilvish on the shoulder.

"Catch hold!" he cried.

The man twisted and grasped, his left hand seizing hold of the belt just above the buckle. Dilvish braced himself and turned as the other slid past.

"Don't let go!" the man cried, his right hand catching hold of the belt above the left as his body slued sideways.

"I wouldn't lose a good belt just for the pleasure of seeing a man in an acid pit," Dilvish answered through clenched teeth, feeling the full weight of the other now. "And it's getting too dark to enjoy the spectacle properly," he continued, drawing the other upward until he could catch hold of his hand.

A greenish glow began in the pool below, and moments later a blinding fountain of sparks rose above it.

"My staff!" the man cried, glancing back over his shoulder. "My staff! You've no idea what went into its crafting—what powers were stored within it!"

"I'll bet your life's worth more," Dilvish said, looping his belt over his neck and catching hold of the man's other hand.

An enormous bubbling began within the now-green pool, and the fumes rose more noxious than before.

The man managed a smile.

"Of course you're right," he said, his boot slipping out from beneath him as he attempted to gain footing. He immediately commenced an almost profound stream of profanity. Dilvish listened with admiration, for even in his military days he would have been hard put to find its equal.

"You managed to blaspheme gods even the priests have forgotten," he said with awe in his voice when the other paused for breath and began coughing. "I owe it to the Art now to drag you out of here. Don't try to stand up. Just let me pull you along to where my mount waits."

Dilvish drew the man up and across the slope, finally raising one of his yellow-tunicked arms and drawing it over his shoulders, assisting him to throw the other across Blaek's back. Behind them, a series of small explosions began within the roiling pool.

"Don't try to keep your footing," Dilvish said. "Just lean and let us carry you. Let your feet drag."

The man stared at Black for a moment and then nodded.

Dilvish and Black resumed their upward progress. Tendrils of fog slid across the darkened sky. The slope shuddered slightly beneath their feet, following another disruption within the pool. Black paused in mid-stride and waited until it had passed.

"That's quite a staff you had there," Dilvish commented.

The man gnashed his teeth and growled. Black's hoofs crunched through the glossy surface.

"It was like an account with an honest banker," the man said finally. "I had invested it with power over the years, against a time of need. Claiming the castle is going to be more difficult without it."

"Sad," said Dilvish. "Why do you want the castle so badly?"

The man only looked at him.

They neared the rim, pausing several more times to allow the passage of intermittent shudders emanating from below. When Dilvish looked back, all that he could see was a welling of greenish foam which now reached fully a third of the way up the sides of the depression. The air was clearer here, however, where a light breeze from the northwest reached them.

They moved steadily up the final distance and mounted the rim. Dilvish dropped his scarf to his neck and refastened his belt when they stood upon level ground. Black snorted a wisp of smoke. The man they had rescued brushed at his black fur leggings. They faced the castle, which was now an inky silhouette against a dusky sky. The sun shone pale as a moon in high heaven.

"If my flasks are not all broken or lost, I'll fix us some wine and water," Dilvish said, moving around to Black's right.

"Good."

"My name is Dilvish."

"I am Weleand of Murcave, and I am beginning to wonder about this place."

"What do you mean?"

"It was my understanding that Tualua, who lies within, had undergone one of his periodic fits of madness—" He gestured widely. "—and so brought all this about with his unbridled energies and his dreaming."

"So it would seem."

"No."

"What, then?"

"Not all dreams are lethal—even those of his kind. Nor are all of them subtle. This entire belt about the castle strikes me as a carefully planned series of defensive deathtraps, not as the mongering wet dreams of a feebleminded demigod."

Dilvish passed him a flask and Weleand took a long pull at it.

"Why—and how—should this be?" he asked.

Weleand lowered the flask and laughed.

"It means, my friend, that someone has already taken control within. He has set this up to keep the rest of us out while he consolidates his power."

Dilvish smiled.

"Or while he recovers his strength," he said. "A tired, injured Jelerak may well have constructed such a defense to keep his enemies at bay."

Weleand took another drink and returned the flask. He wiped his mouth on the back of his hand and stroked his beard.

"It may be as you say, only—"

"What?"

"Only I think not. This sort of thing is too primeval. He would have drunk deeply of this power and been healed. Then he would have had no need for such foolery."

Dilvish sipped at the flask and nodded slowly.

"That, too, may be true—unless he is extremely enfeebled and things have gotten out of hand. It is not unknown for an apprentice to turn upon his master either."

Weleand faced the castle and stared.

"I know of but one way to learn for certain what prevails within," he said at last.

He jammed his hands into pockets in his leggings and began strolling off in the direction of the castle. Dilvish mounted Black and followed slowly after him. He leaned forward and whispered a single word:

"Impressions."

"That man," Black replied softly, "may be a very powerful white sorcerer masquerading as something more sinister. On the other hoof, he may be as dark as my hide—but I do not believe that he is anything in between. And I am sure of the power."

As they moved on, the winds rose again and the mists came up off the ground. They were headed into a forest of tall, bleached, irregularly shaped stones. When they entered it, their footfalls grew silent upon the powdery talc that covered the ground, that swirled in occasional blizzards about them. The wind began to sing among the rocky towers—high-pitched and wavering. Glass flowers tinkled in the shadows of the monoliths' bases. Weleand trudged on, slightly hunched. Streamers of pale fog snaked along the pinnacles. Tiny points of white and orange light appeared, to dance and dart in the middle air. It reminded Dilvish of his recent trek into the far North, yet the temperature was not exceptionally chill. He watched the flapping of Weleand's brown cloak some twenty paces ahead. Abruptly the man halted, pointed off to his right, and laughed.

Dilvish came up beside him and stared. Up a stone alley, partly covered by a drift of talc, a moist-seeming, manlike shape was crouched on both knees and right hand; the left hand was raised, and there was a look of open-mouthed surprise on the upturned face. Moving nearer, Dilvish saw that the apparent moistness was actually a solid glassy sheen with a faint bluish cast to it. He also saw that the figure's trousers were pushed down around the knees.

Dilvish leaned forward and touched the upraised hand.

"A glass statue of a man relieving himself?" he said.

He heard Weleand's chuckle.

"He wasn't always a glass statue," the other stated. "Look at that expression! If we had a little brass plate, we could make him a caption: 'Caught with his pants down when the werewinds blew.'"

"You are familiar with the phenomenon?" Dilvish asked.

"Elimination or werewinds?"

"I'm serious! What happened here?"

"Tualua—or his master—seems to have incorporated the more brittle aspects of a transforming wind into the repertory. Such winds were said to be more common in the early days of the world—the breath of a drunken god, perhaps?—leaving behind such curious artifacts as are occasionally unearthed in the southern deserts. Occasionally, they can be quite amusing—such as this, or a pair once found near Kaladesh, now in the collection of Lord Hyelmot of Kubadad. Several books, now out of circulation, have been written, cataloging—"

"Enough!" said Dilvish. "Is there anything that can be done for the poor fellow?"

"Short of another werewind's coming along and retransforming him, no. And that's not very likely. So help yourself if you want souvenirs. He's very brittle. Here, I'll show you."

He reached toward the figure's ear. Dilvish caught his wrist.

"No. Let him be."

Weleand shrugged and dropped his arm.

"At least it is refreshing to learn that whoever is behind it all has a sense of humor," he remarked.

He turned away then, thrust his hands back into his pockets, and resumed his travel.

Dilvish and Black fell into step behind him again. Long minutes passed and the lights drifted, the wind continued its song unbroken—

"Black! Go left!"

"What is it?"

"Do it!"

Black turned immediately, passing between two pale spires and around a third. He halted.

"Which way?"

"Left. Back farther. I saw it by one of those little lights. I think I saw it . . . Straight ahead now, then right. Back in there."

They slid in and out of shadows. Weleand was lost to sight. One of the lights descended, moved by, transforming a grotesque rock crop they were passing into something else, shining and fair . . .

"Gods!" Dilvish cried, sliding to the ground, moving toward it. "It cannot be—"

He leaned very close, straining his eyes against the shadow which shrouded the figure.

"It—"

He reached out and carefully, almost delicately, touched the face, moving his fingers slowly over the features. Another light moved unsteadily toward them, dropping, retreating, wobbling along. Black, who nearly always stood stock-still when at rest, shifted from foot to foot.

The light steadied, moved forward and upward once again.

"—is!" Dilvish breathed as the glow fell upon the features he caressed.

He fell to his knees and lowered his head for several moments. Then he looked up again, brow furrowed, eyes narrowed.

"But how can it be—here—after all these years?"

Black made a wordless noise and moved forward.

"Dilvish," he said, "what is it? What has happened?"

"In that other life, before the doom was laid upon me," Dilvish said, "long before . . . I—I loved an Elvish maid—Fevera of Mirata. She stands before us. But how can that be? So much time has passed, and this changing land is a recent thing . . . She is unchanged. I—I do not understand. What mad turn of fate can it be—to find one for whom I had given up hope—here, frozen for eternity? I would give anything to restore her."

The wavering point of light had floated away while he spoke, though sunlight pale as that of the moon now fell nearby. Other lights drifted, and a strange shadow moved toward them.

"Anything? Is that what you said?" came the deep and now-familiar voice of Weleand.

The man came forward, seeming taller now in the half-light, and entered the triangle formed by Dilvish, Black, and the statue.

"I thought that you said nothing could be done for such a one," Dilvish stated.

"Under ordinary circumstances, that is true," Weleand replied, reaching out to touch the lady's frozen shoulder, where she stood with her hand upon the bridle of a gleaming horse, looking upward. "However, in view of your extraordinary offer . . ."

His left hand shot forward and fell upon Black's neck.

Black emitted a wail and reared, fires dancing in his eye sockets. Weleand's hand, retaining contact, slid across his chest and onto his wavering leg.

"I know you!" Black cried, and a diminutive bolt of lightning leaped from his mouth, veered away from Weleand and charred the ground nearby.

Then Black grew immobile and the fires died in his eyes. A glossy sheen fled across his hide. The girl sighed and collapsed against her horse. The horse whinnied and moved its feet.

Weleand immediately stepped past Black, turned to face the new tableau, and seized the corners of his cloak behind him as he bowed.

"As you requested," he said, smiling. "One may take the place of another, Lord Dilvish—and in this case, I was able to throw in the lady's horse. You've come out ahead. One good turn, as they say—"

Dilvish rushed forward, but the man was suddenly swept backward and up, as if he were a leaf in the singing wind, to rise, spiraling among the stony towers, cloak extended like a great dark wing behind him, to wheel away to the northeast and out of Dilvish's sight.

He turned toward Black, who stood balanced upon his hind legs, a statue out of dark ice, and he extended his hand. Black swayed and began to topple.

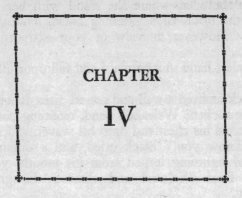

CHAPTER

IV

BARAN of Blackwold paced within the small chamber. Several old volumes lay opened on the table beside the wall. All the paraphernalia for conjuring lay spread upon the floor, and he found his way without glancing down as he walked.

A tall mirror with a grayish cast to its glass hung within an elaborately wrought iron frame, chased about with figures both animal and human, engaged in acts of a mainly violent nature. An elongated orange-gold form swam within the depths of the mirror, as a fish in a shaded pool. It was not a reflection of anything within the room. The paraphernalia had already been used.

"I charge thee, speak," Baran said in a low voice. "You have had ample opportunity to explore the mechanism of the mirror's operation. Tell me of it."

A musical, almost cheerful voice chimed in the vicinity of the glass:

"It is very intricate."

"I already knew that."

"I mean to say that I see how it functions, but I do not understand how the effects were wrought. The spells involved are incredibly subtle."

The figure seemed to be swimming toward the surface. It grew. It turned. Its body was obscured by its shining, elongated head, which rushed forward until it filled the entire glass—triangular-eyed, gilt-scaled, small-mouthed, above a tiny, pointed chin, below a broad forehead, its three small horns thrusting forward from amid a soft and stirring mane of feathers or of flame.

"Release me now," it requested. "It is a doorway to other places, from other places. There is no more that I can tell you."

Baran halted and raised his head, hands clasped behind his back. He regarded it and smiled.

"Try," he said. "Try describing to me the mechanism of its defense. Every guardian I have set within it to prevent its functioning has vanished in a matter of days. Why is this?"

"I find it difficult to suppose. The spells lie dormant now, awaiting the proper key. Yet it is as if there were a stirring within their depths, as if something very cold might be moved to strike to clear the way, should it be blocked."

"Are you capable of blocking it?"

"Yes."

"What would you do if the cold thing struck?"

"I do not like that cold."

"But what could you do?"

"Defend against it with my own fires, if I were here."

"Would such a defense be successful?"

"I know not."

"Could you not explore that aspect of the spell and tell me how to negate it?"

"Alas! It lies too deep."

"I charge you, by all the names which draw you here, remain within the depths of the glass. Prevent its functioning to transport anyone or anything into or out of this place. Defend yourself to the fullest extent of your ability and power against the cold thing, should it move to destroy you or expel you."

"Then I am not to be released?"

"Not at this time."

"I beseech you: reconsider. It is dangerous in here. I do not wish to go the way of the others, who are no more."

"You are trying to tell me that the mirror cannot be blocked for long periods of time?"

"I fear that this may be the case."

"Then tell me this, since you are regarded wise: not long ago, in the Tower of Ice, the one called Ridley succeeded in blocking a mirror such as this indefinitely. How did he manage to defeat its ends?"

"I do not know. Mayhap he employed a guardian far greater than myself to set his will against its workings."

"That would not be practicable. The power involved would have to be enormous—or else his skill of an extraordinary subtlety."

"Either may well have been the case, or both. One hears of that one even in my domain."

Baran shook his head.

"I cannot believe that such skill and force lay within his hands. I once knew him."

"I did not."

Baran shrugged.

"You have heard my charge. Remain within and block the functioning of the key. If you are destroyed in the process, your successor will continue the work. If I lack the skill or the power, I possess an infinite supply of those such as yourself."

"You cannot!" it cried.

Then it began to wail, a rising, ear-filling note.

"Silence! Return to the depths and do as I have bidden you!"

The face spun away, dwindled, diminished, became a darting thing within the mirror. Baran began retrieving his magical gear and stowing it within bins, chests and drawers.

When the room was cleared, he fetched a basket and a chamber pot from an armoire which stood beside the single window. He placed these before the mirror and kicked a small bench into position near them. Then he crossed the chamber and unbolted the door.

"You," he said, when he had opened it. "Get in here."

A young male slave, clad in colorless tunic, leggings and sandals, sidled into the room, eyes darting.

He cringed as Baran reached for his shoulder.

"I'm not going to hurt you—unless you fail to perform your task. In fact, I've provided everything necessary for your comfort." He drew him toward the bench. "There is food and water in that basket. The reason for the pot is that you are not to desert this station for any reason."

The young man nodded quickly.

"Look into that glass and tell me what you see."

"The—the room, sir. And ourselves . . ."

"Look more deeply. There is one thing there which is not present here."

"You mean that little bright thing, moving—way in back?"

"Exactly. Exactly. You must keep your eye on it at all times. Should it vanish, you must come and tell me immediately. You must not go to sleep, no matter what—so I will send another slave to relieve you later, before you grow weary. Do you understand?"

"Yes, m'lord."

"Have you any questions?"

"Supposing you are not in your chambers?"

"Then my man will be. I will keep him informed as to my whereabouts. Is there anything else?"

"No, sir."

Baran returned to the armoire and took out a broom and a fistful of rags. Returning, he cast these down on the floor before the servant.

"Now, brand my words upon your brain, young man, if you dream of one day reaching a respectable old age and dying in your sleep. It is unlikely that the queen will pass this way. In the event that she should, however, you must under no circumstances tell her what you are about, or that I have set you to it. Snatch up those rags, this broom, look guilty. Say that you were set to cleaning this place. Should she inquire further, say that you found this food here and could not contain your hunger. Understood?"

The man nodded again.

"But might she not punish me for this, m'lord?"

"Mayhap," Baran replied, "though it would in no way compare to the agonies I will inflict if you tell her. But should you bear it with fortitude, I will reward you with a better position."

"M'lord!"

Baran clapped him on the shoulder.

"Fear not, I doubt she will be by."

He moved to the table, where he closed the

books, and took them up under his arm before he departed, whistling.

Semirama, wondering what the world was like in this day, beyond the walls of Castle Timeless, beyond the changing land, looked up in her wanderings through halls and galleries to discover that she had found her way back to her own apartments. She seated herself upon a heap of furs atop a heap of cushions, her eyes focusing slowly upon the intricacies carved into an ebony screen across the large chamber. Something aromatic smoldered within a brazier to her left. Tapestries depicting court scenes and hunting scenes covered much of the wall space. The room's six windows were narrow and high. Animal skins lay upon the flagged floors. The bed was large, canopied, of a dark wood crowded with carvings. Semirama fingered the chain about her neck and tasted her bright lower lip. She heard a sandal shuffle—someone moving from the chamber behind the dark screen.

A stout, plain woman, her hair well into the gray of middle years, looked about the right-hand edge of the screen.

"Madame?" she inquired. "I thought I heard you enter."

"You did indeed, Lisha."

"May I fetch you anything, do anything for you?"

Semirama was silent for several moments, considering. "A small glass of the tawny wine from —Bildesh? I forget where it comes from. You know the one I like," she said.

Lisha entered the room and crossed to a cabinet set against the far wall. A clinking of glass ensued. Shortly, she returned with a glass on a silver tray which she set upon a small table to Semirama's right.

"Anything else, ma'am?" she asked.

"No. I think not." She raised the glass and sipped. "Were you ever in love, Lisha?"

The other woman reddened and turned her eyes away.

"I suppose I once was. That was a long while back."

"What happened?"

"He was taken for a soldier, ma'am. Died in his first engagement."

"What did you do?"

"Cried a lot, as I recall. Grew older."

"You know that I was queen long ago in a city that no longer exists? That Jelerak summoned me back from the land of the dead because my family knew the language of the Old Ones, because he needed an interpreter when the one who serves him here began acting strangely?"

"So I heard. I was here the day he called you back. I first saw you that same evening. They brought you to me, still asleep, some hours later, to take care of. It was three days before your eyes focused, before you spoke."

"That long? I never realized. It was only a week later when poor Jelerak went off and we were left to our own devices. So many months ago . . ."

" 'Poor Jelerak'?"

Semirama turned and studied her servant, frowning.

"I find your reaction puzzling. It is not the first time I have met it. He was always a kindly man. You act as if this were not so."

Lisha began to finger her sash. Her eyes darted.

"I'm only a servant here."

"But why this reaction from so many? You can tell me."

"I—I have heard that long ago he was as you have said . . ."

"But that he is no longer?"

Lisha nodded.

"Strange . . . the things that time does to us," Semirama mused. "I had heard things about him, even near my own end. I did not believe them, however. But then, I was too occupied with thoughts of another to pay much heed to such matters. My husband was busy with his concubines and my heart lay elsewhere . . ."

Lisha brightened, her eyes returning to her mistress's face.

"Yes . . ." said Semirama, regarding the designs of the ebony screen, raising her glass for another sip. "I loved a man of the Elvish kind—he who went off to Shoredan and slew the mighty First, Hohorga, against whom even Jelerak had struggled in vain. Selar was his name. He was slain immediately himself, on completion of the deed . . ."

"I have . . . heard of him, ma'am."

"I should have killed myself then, but I did not. I lived for several years afterward. I consoled myself with other lovers. I died in my sleep. Thinking back now, it had to be foul play. My husband, Randel, I suspect. I was weak." She laughed simply. "If I had known I was to be resurrected, I would surely have done it."

She stretched and sighed.

"You may go, Lisha."

The woman did not move.

"You—you would not be thinking of doing yourself harm now—would you, m'lady?"

Semirama smiled.

"Gods bless you, no. Too much time has passed

for such a gesture to have any meaning. I am no longer that girl. I grew a bit weary over other matters, and my mind turned to the foolishness of youth. Go now, and fear not. I wanted a willing ear. That is all."

Lisha nodded and turned.

"If you need anything more, just call."

"I will."

She watched the woman leave. After a time, she drew upon the chain around her neck once again, raising a small, octagonal, bluish metal locket, inlaid with darkened silver. This she opened, to regard the countenance graven within.

It was a full-face view of a young man—long pale hair, slightly sharp-featured, piercing eyes, a short chin-beard, an appearance of strength or determination in the width of the brow, the line of the mouth.

She looked for a moment, touched it to her lips, closed it, let it fall. She finished her drink.

Rising, she wandered about the room, picking up small objects and replacing them. At length, she crossed to the door, found herself again in the hall, stood undecided a moment, began walking.

For over an hour she padded through chambers, along galleries, up and down stairs, meeting no one, occasionally encountering the transitory dreams of her charge, as in the room she found which had been transformed into an undersea grotto, the hall through which a hurricane blew, the corridor blocked with ice, the inky hole in the middle of the air which opened upon nothing, though soft, exotic music emerged from it. At one point, her way was strewn with flowers; at another, with toads. A storm raged within the main hall; a gentle blue rainfall descended within its antechamber.

Gradually, she found her feet turned, climbing, bearing her in the direction of the room of the Pit. But she was of no mind to speak with Tualua now, even in search of memories of times gone by. *Am I the last*, she wondered, not for the first time, *the last person in the world who can converse with him?*

She moved along the gallery outside his chamber. She paused to look out and down. There was a dark area off to her right, as if night had prematurely domed those far rocky acres. To her left, the land was in a state of flux once more, rippling as if under heat waves, upheaving itself, changing colors. The fogs had retreated eastward, where they formed a great yellow wall.

She moved forward and seated herself upon the wide sill, a cushion at her back. There was nothing living in sight below.

What are the cities like now? she thought. *How much have they changed?*

Meliash, at his records, felt rather than heard his name being called. He set aside his writing equipment and fumbled after his crystal.

It cleared almost instantly, and he faced the rheumy-eyed Rawk, who smiled faintly.

"Did I disturb you?" the old man asked.

"No."

"Pity. Well, I've something for you. I found the date in our Book of Signs for that recognition signal. It was somewhat over two hundred years ago. Checking the membership records for the same period, I learned that there was but one person named Dilvish among the Brotherhood—half Elf, House of Selar, a minor adept, appears to have been a military man. I think I might have met him once. Tall fellow, I believe."

"I feel that might well be him. What else have you got?"

"He is gone from the rolls a few years later. No reason given. There is more to it than that, I believe, thinking back. But I can't remember what."

"Try."

"I did. But it seems to be beyond reach."

"What about the other one?"

"The current rolls show a Weleand from the small western town of Murcave. A minor magician. In good standing."

"Of extreme persuasion, either way?"

"No. He's gray."

"Was Dilvish?"

"Yes."

"Have you anything else at all on either of them?"

"Only my curiosity. Do you mind telling me what this is about?"

Meliash leaned back, sorting his feelings, impressions, and ideas. Then he spoke slowly:

"I am bound by this assignment to check into anything peculiar pertaining to . . . the former proprietor of the castle at the center of things. Now, this Dilvish is the only person who has passed this way who has said that he is not seeking the power within the place. Indeed, he has stated that his sole purpose in coming here is to kill . . . the castle's erstwhile lord. He would not elaborate."

"There are many who would like to take vengeance on that one."

"Of course. But Dilvish is the only one who has come calling. Also, he was aware of the business at the Tower of Ice—"

"That is hardly a secret matter any longer within the Society."

"True. But he mentioned having been in the far North recently."

Rawk gnawed at his beard.

"I don't see what you're getting at. I don't recall hearing of any third party being involved in that affair."

"Nor I. But didn't Ridley have a sister?"

"Yes. Pretty thing. Reena, by name. She's a Society member herself."

"It seems I heard she escaped, with some assistance . . ."

"That does sound correct."

"Is there any way we could check further into that?"

"Possibly. There were any number of members watching the conflict—from the safety of their own apartments. Some one of them might have further information."

"Would you try to find out for me?"

Rawk sighed.

"I fail to see what it would prove."

"So do I, at this time. Yet I feel something is there."

"All right. I will inquire of several and let you know what I learn. But what is Weleand's place in all this?"

"I do not know. He came by earlier and warned me of Dilvish's coming, insinuating that he was darker than gray and not to be trusted."

"Something personal, most likely. I will be back when I know more."

His image faded.

Meliash polished the crystal upon his sleeve before replacing it. Then he rose and walked the perimeter of the changing land, where he stood with his hands clasped behind his back, staring off toward the darkened area which had occurred to the southwest.

Dilvish rushed to the side, interposing his shoulder to block Black's passage to the ground.

"What is it? What is happening?" a soft, almost familiar woman's voice inquired.

"Help me!" Dilvish called out, bracing himself, not even looking to where the girl now stood, brushing hair back from her face. "We can't let him fall! Hurry!"

Moments later, she was beside him, her back against Black's left flank.

"Stormbird, come to me—gently," she said, speaking in High Elvish.

The white horse moved toward them.

"Around." She gestured with her head, sliding toward Dilvish.

The horse moved toward the rear, turned.

"Your shoulder, where mine was—lean!"

The horse moved, taking some of Black's weight upon himself. The girl turned toward Dilvish and lapsed into the common tongue:

"What now?" she asked him.

"Down now, to the ground, with great care, lest he shatter," Dilvish replied, speaking High Elvish himself for the first time in many years.

She studied his face for a moment, then nodded.

It took several minutes and one near-catastrophe before Black lay on his side upon the ground.

"I do not understand what is happening," the girl said. "One moment I was standing over there, now it is night and you appear out of nowhere, propping a statue of—it isn't exactly a horse, is it?"

"No," Dilvish replied, turning toward her. "No, Fevera, it is not."

She cocked her head, narrowed her eyes.

"Who are you?" she asked.

"You do not recognize me?"

"I am Arlata of Marinta. Fevera is my grandmother's name."

". . . of the House of Mirata?" Dilvish asked.

"The same. Who are you?"

"Does she still live?"

"Possibly. She went away several years ago, into the Twilit lands. You seem acquainted with the family, but—"

"Forgive me. I am Dilvish of Selar."

"You? The one they say was stricken to stone long ago?"

"The same."

"Is it true?"

"That I was stone? My body was, yes. My spirit was—elsewhere. And you yourself were a statue until a little while ago. Not of stone, but of some glassy substance—as my mount now is."

"I do not understand."

"Nor do I, completely. A sorcerer named Weleand restored you by somehow transferring the effect to Black, here. Do you know anything of such a one?"

"Weleand? No, I've never heard of the man. I was a statue?"

"You and your mount both. Standing over there." He gestured. "You have no memory of how it happened?"

"None." She shook her head slowly. "The last I recall was dismounting here to rest a little before going on. I had but stepped down when the wind acquired a peculiar note. Then it struck me like a wave, and I remember that it was incredibly cold. Then I heard your voice, and it seemed as if I were coming out of a faint or a slumber. I am sorry that your mount was the price of my awakening."

"You had small choice in the matter."

"Still, if there were anything I could do—"

"Don't say that! It was similar words on my part that brought the entire thing about. Talk that way, and Weleand's likely to turn up and change you back."

He looked skyward. She followed his gaze.

"It is a strange moon," she said at last.

"It's the sun."

"What?"

"It is not really night. The darkness is unnatural." He gestured. "And the castle lies that way."

She turned.

"I cannot see it."

"Take my word."

"What is now to be done?" she asked. "I have studied the Art, but I know of no way to restore—" She nodded toward Black. "—that. What is he?"

"That story is too long," Dilvish replied, "and what is done is done. Yet I know not what to do. I cannot leave him this way, and I cannot let you go on alone."

At that moment, a single word echoed within Black's frozen throat:

"Go!" he said.

Dilvish turned and dropped to one knee, placed his head alongside Black's.

"You hear! You can speak!" he cried. "Is there anything at all that I can do for you?"

There was silence for the space of a dozen pulse beats, then Black's voice rang again: "Go!"

Dilvish rose and turned toward Arlata.

"He generally means what he says," he stated, "but I feel worse now than ever. There is no way of telling what new misfortune may pass this way to cause him further distress."

"But he must possess intellect if he speaks—and some power beyond that of our kind, to be able to speak under the circumstances."

"Yes, to both," Dilvish replied. "He is a magical being. He knows things that I do not know. In fact, he can detect an emanation from Tualua before the wave strikes—and I am wondering now whether he was warning of this."

"What, then, should we do?"

"I think we should do as he says—get out of here."

Dilvish turned and pointed.

"Get mounted and head for the castle. I'll follow on foot."

"I believe that Stormbird will carry both of us." She spoke quietly to the horse, and he came up and stood before them. "Mount!"

"I would slow your progress," Dilvish said.

She shook her head.

"We've a better chance together. I'm sure. Mount!"

Dilvish obeyed, and she followed him. She guided Stormbird to the northwest, and Dilvish looked back as they departed, to the place where Black lay like a block of ice.

The sky darkened as they rode, the pale, westering sun growing fainter and fainter. They rode for several minutes, hurrying past two more gleaming human statues at which Dilvish did not look any longer than was necessary to determine that neither was Weleand. The distances between the ghostly stands of stone began to widen. The layer of talc grew thinner and the sounds of Stormbird's hoofbeats began to reach their ears.

Abruptly, the singing winds ceased. Far ahead, a large, open area came into view, where the ground was darker and lightly ridged. Stormbird's pace increased moments before they felt a sharp vibration, followed by a loud explosion from over-head. For several seconds the sky grew bright as day, and then it darkened again.

A little farther along, the way was lightened once more, this time by tiny flakes of fire which began to descend like snow.

At first the flames were falling only ahead and to the right, but soon they were upon them, and Dilvish raised his cloak to shield Arlata and himself. Stormbird whinnied, laid his ears back, and raced beyond the final pinnacles.

"Those glints ahead!" Dilvish cried. "Is it water?"

Arlata's answer, if there was one, was lost to him in the series of explosions which sounded then, above and somewhat to the rear. The falling flames increased in size and number.

"Those last noises sounded almost like laughter of a sort," Arlata called back to him.

Dilvish twisted his body so as not to uncover them to the flames, and looked back. A fiery, man-like outline with a mane of flaming hair towered before the pale, stony land they had just quitted, its silhouettes still visible through the half-substantial form. The figure's right hand was upraised to a great height, and it held a huge bowl of fire from which it shook the blazing leaves that fell upon the land.

"You're right!" Dilvish shouted. "It's an ele-mental—the biggest one I've ever seen!"

"Can you do anything about it?"

"I've never been very good with elementals, except sometimes earth ones. But that looks like water up ahead."

"Yes, it does."

They veered to the right. Dilvish's cloak was

smoldering in a dozen places by then. He smelled burning horsehair as well, and Stormbird was making sharp, nickering noises with increasing frequency.

"The gods know what may be in that water," she said as they reached it, dark and glinting with the reflected light from behind them, "but it can't be much worse than being burned alive."

Dilvish did not reply, but battered at the flames which fell within reach upon them. Another series of explosive peals of laughter sounded above them, much nearer this time. Dilvish looked again and saw that the elemental was almost upon them—and even as he watched, it upended the bowl and an unbroken stream of fire poured forth like bright honey.

"Ride! He's dumping it all! Right on us!" he cried.

Arlata shouted to Stormbird, and the horse put forth a final effort, leaping about like one of the great white cats of the snowfields. The fires fell almost directly behind them and splattered. Dilvish took his long gauntlets into his hand and began beating at Stormbird's tail, at the two places where the hair was burning.

Then water was splashing all about them, and the pace was slowed and Dilvish felt his legs grow wet up to the knees. He restored his gloves to his belt, leaned forward, and dropped his cloak back over his shoulders, for the firefall had ended.

They splashed on ahead and the water grew no deeper. After a time it even grew shallower, though the bottom became mucky as they progressed. It was still and very cold. When Dilvish looked back again, he saw that the elemental had retreated into the still, pale forest of stone, and only its flowing, flaming mane and blazing shoulders were visible as it moved away.

He could not understand a feeling that something was out of joint until he realized that though the flames were dead, the world seemed no darker than it had been. In fact, it appeared to be lightening. He regarded the sky and realized that the moonlike sun had brightened. Looking ahead then, he saw that the area before them was lighter still, with a pearly complexion upon the face of the water. Moving beyond twilight, the world began to brighten with almost every sucking pace they advanced. The hazy outline of the Castle Timeless loomed large suddenly, immediately before and above, its windows like the dark eyes of an enormous insect.

"I see the shore now!" Arlata announced. "It is not all that far ahead. Stormbird can rest . . ."

For the first time, Dilvish became aware of all the places where their bodies touched.

"You were a soldier, weren't you?" she asked.

"For a time."

"Not just in the old days. There was some engagement within the past few years."

"Yes. We won and I've done with all that. I set out on a personal quest after the last battle. I stop and work occasionally at anything available, replenish my supplies, and continue on."

"What is it that you seek?"

"The man who turned me to stone and sent me to Hell."

"Who might that be?"

Dilvish laughed.

"Why else would I journey through this nightmare? The man whose castle lies ahead, of course."

"Jel—the old wizard? I've heard he is dead."

"He is not dead—yet."

"So we are not in competition for the power of Tualua?"

"You can have Tualua. Just leave me his master."

"Obviously, you intend to kill him."

"Of course."

"You may be wasting your time. I inquired before I came this way. In the opinion of Wishlar of the Marshes, he is not here. He felt that he might even be dead. That was why I thought so."

"Wishlar still lives? I knew him when I was a boy. Is he at Ban-Selar still?"

"Yes, though that area has been annexed by Orlet Vargesh and is no longer known by the old name. Oh . . . that would have been your family, would it not?"

"Yes. When I've settled this business, I'd like to set those claims right. If you see this—Orlet—before I do, tell him that I said so."

"Dilvish, if the one you seek be indeed within, I've a feeling you might not be traveling home."

"Most likely you're right. But I'll be happy to go if I can take him along with me."

"I've often heard it said that a strong hatred is self-destructive. Now I believe it."

"I like to think that I'll be doing good for a lot of others as well as for myself, should I succeed."

"But if that were not the case, would you still do it?"

"Yes."

"I see."

Stormbird slowed as they drew nearer the shore.

"A magician of that power could blast you with a look," she said.

"Black was to have helped me on that count. I met him in Hell. But even without him, I know that Jelerak is weaker now than perhaps he ever has been. And I bring weapons I believe are more than sufficient to the task."

Stormbird uttered a long neighing sound and halted, panting.

"We've tired him to the end of endurance," she said, dismounting. "Let us lead him ashore."

"Yes," Dilvish replied, swinging his leg and stepping down. "He needs a rubdown, he needs my cloak. We can rest for a—"

The neighing continued. The horse appeared to be struggling now, and there was foam upon his lips.

"I—"

Dilvish sank into the mud. He struggled to raise his foot, failed.

"Oh, no! I have come so far—" she said, looking ahead to where the bright sun shone upon a clear, sandy shore, to where the grasses waved beyond it, where patches of blue and red flowers swayed within the field.

She lowered her head and Dilvish heard her sob.

"It isn't fair," she said.

Dilvish struggled, leaned forward, wrapped his arms around her.

"What are you doing?"

He dragged, lifted. Slowly she began to rise. The water grew muddy about them. Bubbles broke on the surface. She came higher within his arms as he sank lower.

"Reach for Stormbird," he said, twisting his body. "Get onto him."

She extended her arms, caught hold of the horse's mane with her left hand, cast her right across his back. Still sinking, Dilvish pushed, thrusting her up and forward. She drew herself across the horse's back, threw a muddy and soaking leg over him, rose erect.

"Rest. Recover your strength," Dilvish said, "then swim to shore."

She spoke to Stormbird and caressed him. His struggling ceased. He stood still. Then she leaned to the side, to reach for Dilvish. The distance was too great.

"No good," he said. "You can't help me that way. But when you get ashore, there are those trees off to the left . . . Use your blade. Cut a long limb. Bring it back. Push it out to me."

"Yes," she said, unfastening her cloak. She paused and looked at it. "If you took hold of one end of my cloak, perhaps I could pull you up here."

"Or perhaps I'd pull you back in. No. Do it from the shore. I seem to be stabilizing."

"Wait . . . Supposing I cut my cloak and knot the lengths together? You could take one end and tie it under your arms. I could swim to shore with the other end and try pulling you out as soon as I've a foothold."

Dilvish nodded slowly.

"It may work."

She drew her blade and began cutting the long cloak into strips.

"Now I remember hearing of you," she said as she worked, "as someone who lived long ago. It is a strange feeling, seeing you here and recalling that you loved my grandmother."

"What did you hear about me?"

"You sang, you wrote poetry, danced, hunted. Not the sort of person one would guess to become a Colonel in the Armies of the East. Why did you leave and take up such a life? Was it grandmother?"

Dilvish smiled faintly.

"Or wanderlust? Or both?" he said. "That was

a long time ago. Memories grow rusty. Why do you want the power that lies in that pile of colored rock up ahead?"

"I could do much good with it. The world is full of evils that cry out for righting."

She finished cutting and sheathed her blade. She began knotting the lengths of cloth together.

"I felt that way once," Dilvish said. "I even tried righting a few. The world is still pretty much the same as it has always been."

"But you are here to try again."

"I suppose . . . But I cannot lie to myself about it. My feelings are not unalloyed. It is as much a matter of revenge for me as it is the removal of an evil from the world."

"I'd guess it's even sweeter when they come together that way."

Dilvish laughed harshly.

"No. My feelings are not such nice things. You don't even want to know them. Listen, if you were to gain the power you seek and try the things you wish to try with it, it will change you—"

"I expect so. I hope so."

"But not in all of the ways you anticipate, I'm sure. It is not always easy to tell an evil from a good, or to separate the two. You would be bound to make mistakes."

"You're certain about what you are doing."

"That's different, and I'm not entirely pleased with it. I feel it has to be done, but I do not like what it is doing to me. Perhaps I would like to dance and sing again one day—when we get out of this. To turn around and go home."

"Would you come with me?"

Dilvish looked away.

"I can't."

She smiled, coiling her handiwork.

"There. All knotted. Catch the end, now."

She tossed it to Dilvish, who snagged it, passed it under his arm, around his back and forward beneath his other armpit. He knotted it before him.

"Good," she said, securing the other end at her waist and slinging her blade across her back. "When we're both ashore, one of us can swim back and put a line on Stormbird. The two of us will drag him loose."

"I hope so."

She leaned forward and spoke again to the horse, stroking his neck. He nickered and tossed his head but did not struggle.

"All right," she announced, drawing up her feet, rising into a crouched position on Stormbird's back, one hand still twisted in his mane for balance.

She released her grip and drew her arms back.

"Now!" she said.

Her arms shot forward, her legs straightened. She cut the water in a powerful plunge which bore her almost entirely to the shore before she took a single stroke.

Then her arms moved a few times. She raised her head and moved to rise. She screamed:

"I'm sinking!"

Dilvish began drawing back on the slack line which joined them, to pull her into the water. She was over her knees in the sand-encrusted mud, and still sinking rapidly.

"Don't struggle," Dilvish said, finally drawing the line taut. "Take hold with both hands."

She gripped it and leaned forward. Dilvish began to haul upon it, slowly, steadily. She ceased sinking, bent far forward.

Then, with a single, sharp noise, the line parted and she fell face forward.

"Arlata!"

She struggled upright again, face and hair splashed with mud. Dilvish heard her utter a single sob as she began sinking once more. He cursed softly, the slack line still in his hands.

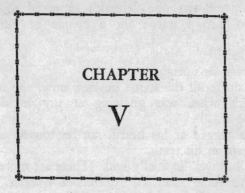

CHAPTER

V

"Please, sir, how is a girl to rest when you keep jumping into and out of bed with such annoying frequency?" said the dark-eyed girl through the pale screen of her hair.

"Sorry," said Rawk, brushing the hair aside to stroke her cheek. "It's this damned Society business that's come up. I keep thinking of records I should be checking. I get up to check them, I find nothing, I re-retire."

"What seems to be the problem?"

"Mm. Nothing you could help me with, my dear." He dropped his clawlike hand upon her shoulder. "I'm trying to find more information on this Dilvish fellow."

"Dilvish the Deliverer, the hero of Portaroy?" she asked. "He who raised the lost legions of Shoredan to save the city a second time?"

"What? What are you saying? When was this?"

"A little over a year ago, I believe. Also known as Dilvish the Damned, in a popular ballad of the same name—the one Jelerak's supposed to have turned into a statue for a couple of hundred years?"

"Gods!"

Rawk sat upright.

"I do recall the statue business now," he stated. "That's what was gnawing at my mind! Of course . . ."

He tugged at his beard, ran his tongue among the gaps in his teeth.

"Oh, my!" he finally said. "There are more sides to this thing than I'd realized. I wonder, then, what that Weleand fellow would have against such a one. If he has a contact file, I've a mind to ask him. Might as well get the whole picture before I report back."

He leaned over and brushed his lips against her cheek.

"Thank you, my pigeon."

He was out of bed and down the hall, nightshirt flapping.

He rushed across the great Society library to a large, nondescript piece of furniture. Finally, he began rummaging in one of its drawers. After a time he straightened, bearing in his hand an envelope across which the name "Weleand" was written.

Opening the envelope, he discovered it to contain several strands of white hair, held together by a drop of red sealing wax.

These he removed and took with him to the black-hung table in the corner, where he deposited them beside a yellow ball of crystal. Then he seated himself and stared forward, lips moving, fingers touching the white strands.

Shortly, the crystal clouded. It remained so for a time. Rawk began repeating the name "Weleand." Finally, there came a clearing. A fat-faced, nearly bald man peered up at him. He seemed out of breath.

"Yes?" he inquired.

"I'm Rawk, Society Archivist," Rawk stated. "I'm sorry to trouble you in the midst of such an arduous undertaking, but there is something you might be able to clarify for us."

The man's brow furrowed.

"Arduous undertaking?" he said. "It's just a little spell—"

"You needn't be modest."

"—of interest mainly to practitioners of veterinary sorcery. Of course, I'm rather proud of what it does for the mange."

"Mange?"

"Mange."

"I—Aren't you in the foothills of the Kannais, in the changing belt, near the Castle Timeless?"

"I'm treating a stable of ailing horses here in Murcave. Is this a joke?"

"If it is, it is on us, not on yourself. Do you know anything at all about a man named Dilvish, who rides a metal horse?"

"His reputation only," Weleand replied. "He is said to have played a significant role in one of the border wars awhile back—at Portaroy, I believe. I've never met him."

"You've not spoken with a Society representative named Meliash recently, have you?"

The other shook his head.

"I know who he is, but I've never met him either."

"Oh. Then we have been fooled—by someone, about something. I'm not certain who, or what. Thank you for your time. I'm sorry to have bothered you."

"Wait! I would at least like to know what is happening."

"So would I. Someone—a fellow of the Art—used your name recently. Down South. He is apparently not kindly disposed to this Dilvish, who is also down there. I can't say that I understand what it all means."

Weleand shook his head.

"Rivals, most likely," he said, "and the one using my name is doubtless up to no good. Let me know what comes of this, will you? I've a good reputation, and I don't want it besmirched."

"I'll do that. Good luck with the mange."

"Thank you."

The crystal clouded again and Rawk sat staring into its depths, trying to order his thoughts. Finally, he rose and returned to bed.

Dreaming dreams of days gone by and wondering at the bright world beyond, Semirama regarded the changing land. It was about time for another wave—one of massive destructiveness—to sweep over it. She smiled. Things were working according to plan. Once matters were resolved here, she could go forth to enjoy the present incarnation of the world. What sort of garments might now be in fashion? she wondered.

Below, she saw two figures on horseback emerge from the darkened area, splashing across the still waters of the treacherous pond.

Why did they keep coming? she wondered. Nothing had changed here, so they must be aware that all of their predecessors had failed. Avarice and stupidity, she decided. All noble sentiments had doubtless vanished with her own times. Still—

There!

The horse was stuck, near to the shore. Two

more power-hungry fortune-seekers were about to enrich the world with their absence.

Idly, she leaned forward and ran her hand along the side of the window, pronouncing the spell of activation, directing its focus toward the couple on the horse.

The scene leaped forward and Semirama's face underwent a series of rapid changes. She touched the window again, with additional words of fine tuning.

The Elfin girl was common enough. One of the willowy blonde sort, from Marint' or Mirat'. But the man—

"Selar!" she gasped, her hand moving to her throat, eyes wide. "Selar . . ."

The girl had dismounted. The man was following her.

"No!"

Semirama had risen to her feet. Her fists were clenched at her sides. Both figures were now in the water, beginning to struggle. And—something else . . .

The change wave! It was beginning!

Turning, she ran toward the Chamber of the Pit, phrases in the chirping tongue of the Old Ones already rising to her lips. As she entered the reeking room, she saw the demon Baran had quieted earlier, lurking in a corner, gnawing on a bone.

She snapped several brief words in Mabrahoring at it, and it cringed. She reached the edge of the pit and warbled three vibrant notes. After several moments, she repeated them. A dark, amorphous form broke the shadowy surface and writhed slowly. It emitted a single musical tone. She responded with an intricate aria to which she received a very brief reply.

She sighed then and smiled. They exchanged a

few more notes. Then a tentacle rose beside her and she embraced it. She held it for a long while, unmoving, and gradually her flesh took on a faint glow.

When she finally released it with a parting note and turned away, she looked somehow larger, stronger, wilder. Her eyes flashed as she approached the demon in the corner. It dropped its bone and crouched when she pointed her finger at it, its mismatched eyes rolling and darting.

"That way," she said, indicating the gallery she had recently quitted. "Stay with me."

It moved to obey, but when they had passed through the doorway, it broke into a lop-legged run. She raised her finger again, and this time a line of something like fire seemed to race from it to envelop the creature. Her peculiar aura was diminished slightly as this occurred.

The demon had halted and begun wailing. She crooked her finger and the flames vanished.

"Now you must do as I say," she said, approaching it. "Do you understand?"

It prostrated itself before her, took gentle hold of her right ankle, and placed her foot upon its head.

"Very good," she observed. "One should always define a relationship at the outset." She removed her foot to the ground. "Get up. I want you to accompany me to the window. There is something you must see."

She returned to her former observation post and looked down. The girl was now floundering at the shore's edge and the man was still in the water, by the horse, immersed to near shoulder level. The girl had sunk to a point slightly above her waist.

"Do you see that man in the green kerchief, beside the horse?" she asked. When the demon grunted an affirmative, "I want him," she said.

She reached out and laid her hand upon the creature's head.

"I lay this geas upon you, that you know no rest until you have retrieved him and brought him to me, alive and unmaimed."

The demon drew back.

"But—I—will—sink—too," it rumbled, beginning to tremble. "And—I—do—not—like—water," it added.

She laughed.

"You have my sympathy, for what it's worth," she said. "Still, I see the necessity for something a bit firmer."

She turned toward the center of the gallery, to where the wheelbarrows and carts passed with their burdens from the stable. She looked up and down the hall, then moved off to her left to a place where the fallen dirt from the wheels was deepest. Shaking out a handkerchief, she stooped, spread it flat upon the floor, and began filling it with handfuls of powdered soil. When a good-sized heap was accumulated at its center, she placed her fingertip atop it. More of the spectral light seemed to pass out of her. She looked smaller, less elemental, more human once again. The sandy pyramid, however, was now glowing faintly.

She raised the corners of the handkerchief and knotted them together. Then she turned and held it before the creature.

"Now hear me," she said. "You are to take this with you. When you reach the place where the sinking sands begin, cast some of this before you upon them. It will freeze them to a great depth, so that you may walk on them. Do likewise upon the water and you will fashion yourself a bridge of ice that you may pass over. You need not fear to handle it, however, as long as you are fairly quick about it. It will not work nearly so well on living things. Still, it would be prudent to carry it—so. Take it!"

A taloned hand came forward and took hold of it by the knot.

"If he struggles and does not wish to accompany you," she added, "you may render him unconscious with a sharp blow here—on the bone just behind the ear. Do not strike so hard that you smash the skull, however. Remember that I want him alive and unbroken."

She turned away.

"Follow me, now. You shall depart from the small sitting room to the side of the main hall. That area should be vacant this time of day. Let us hurry!"

Nothing else of a peculiar nature was now occurring anywhere within the castle or its environs. And Semirama had lost her glow.

Baran ordered a large meal prepared, to be served in his apartments, and strolled out while he waited for this to be done. He thought of Semirama again, this time as a confidante and source of information on Jelerak in his earlier days, rather than as a prospective lover. He mounted to the third floor, paused outside her door, adjusted his apparel, and knocked.

Presently, Lisha opened it.

"Is your mistress in?" he inquired.

Lisha shook her head.

"She's walked out. I'm not certain where to, or when she'll be returning."

Baran nodded.

"When she does," he said, "tell her I stopped

by to continue an earlier discussion I still feel
might prove profitable."

"I'll do that, sir."

He turned away. The food would not be ready
for some time yet.

He mounted more stairs, coming at last to the
room where the slave sat bolt upright before the
mirror, staring.

"Any changes?" he asked.

"No, sir. It's still there."

"Very good."

He closed the door, moved to the stairs, and
began to descend. He chuckled for a moment, then
frowned.

*If I can just keep the old bastard out long enough
to get control of Tualua, I'll let him in, then challenge him. If he doesn't show, I'll go looking for
him. Once he's out of the way, even the Society
will step warily about my shadow. I suppose I
could smash them then. Maybe not, though . . .
Even he never tried that. On the other hand, they
do have their uses. Maybe that's it. I wonder how
I'd like heading the group myself . . . ?*

He paused to lean upon a railing, looking out
over a deep, high-ceilinged room with doors at
various heights in its walls, leading nowhere, half-
stairways wandering into nothingness, a dry fountain at its center. As with so many other things
about the castle, he had never been able to figure
its function. It struck him then that Jelerak must
have known of these and many other matters he
might never know. In that moment he was afraid,
and he felt a sudden dizziness which caused him
to draw back from the rail.

*What if she knows? What if Semirama already
has the key, holds the power, and is just toying with*

me—only pretending that all these communications difficulties exist?

He resumed walking down the stair, his hand upon the wall, face averted from the railing.

And who could tell? She must be the only human left in the world who can talk that lingo. Even Jelerak never knew much of it. Never needed to. Had his spells to control the thing. Till it went wild. Wouldn't have used the massive, complicated rites it took to bring her back if he could understand, could talk to it. Ugly, slippery thing, swimming in shit. Probably eats it, too. Ha! Hereditary thing with that family. Priests and priestesses of the Old Ones. They must have known a lot we don't hear about, even sorcerers. Probably as wily and mean as their charges. Powers, too. Don't get her mad unless you know for sure. Might feed you to it.

He pressed nearer to the wall.

But if she knows, has control, what is she waiting for? It's a deep game if that's the case. Was she the last of her line? Have to look that up. Strange thought now . . . Why her, if he could call back anyone he wanted of that family? Knew her in the old days, that's why. Wonder how well? Never thought of the old sack of sticks riding anything but a broom, but he was young once, too . . . Goes in and out in all the right places, she does. Had a pretty lusty reign, too, I believe. Like to surprise her one day with the Hand . . . Wonder if they used to do it and that's why her . . . ?

He reached a landing, took a turn, stopped and shuddered.

Steep stairs, those. Dark. Haven't been this way in ages, though . . .

He seated himself on the top step, moved his feet down, lowered himself to the second step, moved his feet down. His face was wet and his teeth were clenched.

Not since I fell out of the tree, mother! Why now? So long it's been . . . Don't let anyone come by now, see me . . . Oh, my!

He continued inching his way down the stairs.

Think of something else, make it easier . . .

He moved his legs, his hands, his rump; dropped. Again . . .

Supposing, then, it is true? Supposing she has things well in hand and is merely waiting for the return of her old lover? Supposing all of the—effects—are mere trumpery? For my benefit? Each day I stick my neck out a little farther. She smiles and nods and leads me on. Then when Jelerak returns he'll have me howling in some special Hell . . . Just supposing . . .

Another step. He paused to wipe his palms on his sleeves.

Supposing. Just supposing . . . If it is all true, what is to be done?

Another step. Again. He rested his cheek against the wall. His breathing was heavy.

I must keep him out until I am strong. How? Double the guard on the mirror? Set traps and dismiss the spirit? Let him come through and destroy him immediately? Only it might not work. That way I lose, too. There must be something else I can do . . . What a time to have one of these spells! It's been years . . .

He commenced his downward motion once again. The landing was now in sight.

Of course, it is not all that probable. Only a guess, really. He could have his choice among the queens of Hell. Probably has, too . . . On the other hand, she has disdained me on several oc-

*casions. Why else would she do a thing like that,
save that she is being faithful to him?*

Three more steps, quickly. Pause to rest again.

*If I knew for certain there was a secret to be
wrested from her, I would do it. Then all else
would be given to me . . . Strange! How quiet this
place has become! I only just now noticed . . .
What might it be?*

He bounced down the final stairs quickly and
rose to his feet, steadying himself against the railing.

Finally, *I'll go and have a look at big ugly's pit,*
he decided. *He seems to be at the center of everything.*

He pushed himself away and lurched off toward
the gallery.

Then a good dinner to set things right.

Meliash sat upon a hilltop at some distance from
his camp, studying the entire prospect. The changing land had stopped changing. The fogs had dis-
sipated, the winds had died, the landscape was
utterly still. He could view much of the vast wasteland now, frozen into contorted shapes, sweeping
on a full league toward the castle, now sharp-edged
in silhouette by the declining sun. He sought after
any trace of activity within that place but detected
none.

It would seem, he decided, that his superior in
this matter—Holrun—should be notified, and if he
were unavailable, some other member of the Council. It would be good to have something more to
report, however, other than the bare fact that the
turmoil had ceased. If only he possessed some
means of accounting for its quiescence . . .

He was loath to journey forward personally,
lest it suddenly resume its activity. This was neither

a matter of cowardice nor prudence upon his part. The fainthearted had not been considered for this assignment, neither had the impetuous nor the overly cautious. The maintenance of the posts was paramount. It was very likely that, if properly manned, they could contain even the most violent upheavals of the one within, should its excesses rush to overwhelm the boundaries they had established about the domain. The wardens had been selected for their sense of duty, their dedication to what could be a difficult task. Meliash did not wish to depart too far from the place where the black wand was planted.

He sighed and withdrew his crystal. The time had come to tell Holrun this much, anyway. Perhaps the other might even have a suggestion. Perhaps the Council itself might be moved to penetrate the place, on one plane or another, for a quick reconnaissance. He rather doubted they would do this immediately, however. They were still so touchy concerning anything that smelled of Jelerak . . .

As he polished the crystal on his sleeve, he wondered what had become of all those he had seen on their way to the interior. It could well be that one of them had made it through and somehow effected this . . . stillness.

He placed the amber globe on his lap and stared down upon it. The cloudiness was already present within it. He tried to blank his mind and reach out, but it was difficult. His head began to ache. He broke off the attempt at contact. Immediately, the crystal cleared and old Rawk grinned up at him.

"You've got a pained expression, son. Something the matter?"

"Possibly," Meliash replied. "I see what it was

with the crystal, anyway. Have you got something for me?"

"It seems that I do, if my lady has just kicked me out of bed to tell you about it. Why do we put up with it?"

"A wise man may reverse the obvious. Then again, maybe not. What is her message?"

"First, to tell you that the one who passed your post under the name of Weleand was lying. I spoke with the real Weleand earlier. He is in a stable in Murcave, keeping company with sick horses. Next, there is a possibility that your Dilvish is the one Jelerak turned to a stone at about the time ours vanished in the old records. That one was supposed to have been restored recently and distinguished himself in a border clash at Portaroy by raising the legions of Shoredan to succor that city. There is even a song going around. She sang it before she kicked me out of bed. It mentions a metal horse named Black, and it hints of a continuing feud with the sorcerer."

"I am happy that you listened to her."

"It *was* a rousing song— Now, if you will excuse me—"

"Wait. What do you think about this?"

"Oh, she's probably right. She usually is. Her suspicions, though, are a trifle melodramatic."

"I'd like them, anyhow."

Rawk wiped a bit of spittle from the corner of his mouth.

"Well, I'm sure it will give you a good laugh. It did me. She thinks Weleand is Jelerak in disguise and that he is trying to break into his own castle, that he is too weak from his recent injuries up North to employ his usual high-powered means."

"How does she know what happened up North?"

"I talk in my sleep. Anyway, he knows this Dilvish is after him, she says, which is why he said what he did to you—hoping you'd slow his enemy a bit. What can you do with a woman like that?"

"Offer her your job," Meliash said.

"You think there is something to it?"

"The possibility cannot be dismissed. If there is anything to it at all, I think that we—Well. Who knows? Thank her for me. And thank you."

"Glad to be of help. By the way . . ."

"Yes?"

"If you meet this Dilvish again, tell him he's behind on his dues."

Rawk ended the communication and Meliash returned his gaze to the towers of Timeless. That place was another thing on which he wanted information. No time now, though.

Melbriniononsadsazzersteldregandishfeltselior had seldom been exploited by terrestrial adepts, inasmuch as the use of a demon's name was necessary in those rites binding him to servitude. One missed syllable and the conjurer would step from the circle smiling, to discover that the demon was smiling also.

Then, leaving the remains artistically disposed about the conjuring area, the demon would return to the infernal regions, perhaps bearing with him some small souvenir of an amusing interlude.

It was Melbriniononsadsazzersteldregandishfeltselior's misfortune, however, that Baran of the Extra Hand hailed from Blackwold, where a complex, agglutinative language was spoken. This was why he found himself in service to the inhabitants of the Castle Timeless—a precariously moored temporal artifact which frightened him even beyond most things in his homeland. Which was why he was now picking his way downslope across the broken landscape, on a mission toward that sticky area he had thus far been able to avoid, at the behest of the woman he feared above all beings on this plane because of the company she kept. And this was why he feared failure even more than the wear and strain on his mismatched legs, amazingly adapted as they were to the peculiar features of his own little corner of an unusual place.

When he cursed, it sounded like the most pious mouthings of the devout translated into Mabrahoring. And he was cursing now, for the way was rocky and steep. He clutched at the kerchief and rehearsed his instructions as he advanced upon the now-peaceful pond, still portions of humans and a horse jutting above its surface like chess pieces on a blue tabletop.

He was to fetch her one of the humans. Yes. The man. Farther out . . .

He passed the stand of trees, passed the place where the beach began, moved along its periphery. When he came opposite the stuck people, he paused to undo the kerchief. The humans, having caught sight of him, were now shouting to one another. He wondered whether he was permitted to eat the one he was not required to take back—or the horse. He recalled the urgency in Semirama's voice, however, and decided that it would be prudent to forgo either pleasure.

Scooping up a handful of the icy dust, he cast it before him upon the beach and watched as the sands puckered and cracked. He tested the area, found that it bore his weight, and advanced.

He grinned at the girl as he drew near, then halted. He could not pass by her. It was as if an invisible wall barred his way. He extended his sensory equipment over several adjacent planes then, at last determining that she was shielded by a number of protective spells having an effective range of a little over a six-foot radius. He cursed in Mabrahoring and took up more of the sand to arrange for a detour. All he had wanted was a single, decent bite out of her right shoulder.

He sowed the grains before him, passed around the girl, cast more out over the water, and listened to the rapid clicking notes as a bridge of ice formed before him. Abruptly, he halted, extending his senses again. There was something about the position of the man's shoulders that bothered him. Also, though he knew it to be impossible, the face seemed somehow familiar . . .

Aha! He detected the metal. The man was holding a drawn blade out of sight beneath the water.

He took up another handful of dust and hesitated. If he froze the man in that position, he would have to chip him free later. That would never do, especially when the lady wanted quick delivery.

He cast the glowing grains off to his left in an arc curving outward about the man, just beyond full reach of arm and blade. He danced along it as soon as the way was firm, taking up another handful of the dirt, continuing the arc toward a position at the man's back, watching the eyes that watched him, in that face . . .

"Grin, hyena!" the man said in perfect Mabrahoring. "Stump along. I'm almost yours, but not quite. Not yet. One slip and I'll send you home in a hurry. Look down! The ice gives way!"

The demon flailed about, swayed, dropped forward, caught himself with an extended hand, glared at the man before rising again.

"That was well done," he acknowledged. "I would love to eat your heart. You speak well, too. Do you know the Tel Talionis?"

"Yes."

"Doubly sad. For I would enjoy conversing with you."

With that, he leaped to the end of the icy bridge, to the rear of the man, and struck him with a horny knuckle on the bone behind the ear, as he had been instructed.

He seized the man's hair as he slumped forward, then caught hold of him beneath the armpits and began drawing him upward. The water darkened and bubbled as he pulled him free. He slung him across his back, then turned and made his way shoreward, still grinning.

The girl was shouting Elfin pleas and insults at him. As he passed, he looked wistfully at her shoulder. So near and yet so distant . . .

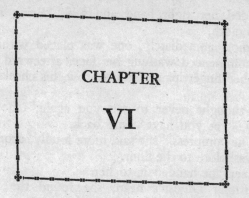

CHAPTER

VI

SEMIRAMA had rung for servants as soon as the demon had departed upon the errand. When, in due course, one arrived in the small room off the main hall, she dispatched him after others, to return with cloths and basins of water, towels, food, wine, a dry robe, and medicines for a cold compress, with particular regard to haste and secrecy.

These had all arrived and were distributed about a couch covered in pale Eastern silks when the demon returned, lurching into the room with Dilvish over one shoulder. The servants drew back in alarm.

"Place him upon the couch," she ordered. Then, to the servants, "You, clean the mud off his boots and trousers. You, bring me the compress," she said. "You, open the wine."

The demon lowered Dilvish to the sofa, then retired across the room. Semirama stared down at the man's face, then slowly seated herself and took his head into her lap. Without looking away, she

111

extended her right hand and said, "Bring me a damp cloth."

Almost immediately, one was placed within it. She commenced washing his face, afterward running her fingertips across his brow, his cheeks, his chin.

"I thought never to see you again," she said softly, "yet you have come back.

"The compress," she said more loudly, dropping the washcloth to the floor.

A servant handed it to her.

Turning Dilvish's head, she found the place where he had been stricken, glared once at the demon, unfolded and refolded the pungent cloth and applied it behind his ear.

"You, wipe off his scabbard, his belt buckle. You, pour some of that wine upon a clean cloth and bring it here."

She was wiping his lips with the wine-cloth when Baran stepped into the room.

"Just what is the occasion?" he demanded. "Who is this man?"

Semirama looked up suddenly, eyes wide. The servants drew back. Melbriniononsadsazzersteldregandishfeltselior crouched in a corner, in awe of Baran's linguistic abilities.

"Why—he is one of the many who have come this way," she said, "seeking, I suppose, the power of the place."

Baran laughed harshly and stepped forward, his hand moving to the hilt of a short blade at his belt.

"Well, let us show him some power by dispatching him and removing another nuisance."

"He has come to us alive," she said steadily. "He should be preserved for your master's judgment."

Baran halted, reviving an earlier train of thought. But then he laughed again.

"But why not let a demon eat him now?" he said. "Why make the poor fellow walk all the way to the prison chamber?"

"What do you mean?" she asked.

"Surely you must know where they get those dainties they're always feasting upon?"

She raised a hand to her mouth.

"I'd never thought about it. The prisoners?"

"The same."

"That should not be. We are supposed to be their jailers."

Baran shrugged.

"This is a big castle in a rough world."

"They are your demons," she said. "Speak to them about it."

He started to laugh again, but then he saw the look in her eyes and he felt a momentary touch of a power that he did not understand. He thought again of her and of Jelerak, and a moment of his earlier vertigo returned.

"I'll do that," he said, and he looked down upon the man, studying him.

"You know why I am here?" he asked. "I was walking in the gallery. You left the window focused upon the pond. I wonder at your rescuing the man and leaving the woman behind. He *is* a good-looking fellow, isn't he?"

For the first time in countless centuries, Semi-rama blushed. Seeing this, Baran smiled.

"It is a shame to waste them," he added.

Then he turned toward the demon.

"Return to the pond," he ordered in Mabra-horing. "Bring me the woman. I could use a little recreation myself."

The demon beat his breast and bowed until his head touched the floor.

"Master, she is defended by a spell against those

such as myself," he said. "I could not draw near her."

Baran frowned. A memory of Arlata's profile stirred within his mind for the first time.

"Very well. I'll get her myself," he said.

He crossed the chamber and flung the door wide. Seven shallow steps led down to a walkway. He took them quickly and departed the walk moments after that, moving toward the edge of the slope the demon had descended earlier.

The sun had fallen into the west. It was already behind the castle and the long shadows had merged before him, casting the fore-edge of twilight's cloak across the steep and rocky way. Baran took several steps forward, to the place where the slope dropped sharply.

He moved to the lee of a large stone and stood with his back against it, looking down. He stared as if hypnotized. He muttered a charm, but it did no good. The prospect seemed to swim before him.

"Not such a good idea," he muttered, breathing heavily. ". . . no. The hell with her. It's not worth it."

Still, he stood as if glued to the stone. The rocks seemed sharper than they had moments before, seemed almost to be reaching for him.

What am I waiting for? Just go back and say it's not worth the trouble . . .

His right foot twitched. He closed his eyes and drew a deep breath. His lust and anger had died. He thought again of the girl trapped below. Her face troubled him. It was not just her beauty . . .

A tiny spark of nobility he would have sworn had never existed, or at least had been extinguished years before, flickered within his breast. He opened his eyes and shuddered as he looked down again.

"All right, damn it! Go get her."

He pushed away from the walk and began walking.

Not quite as bad as it looks. Still . . .

He had descended about forty feet before his way took a turn, and he paused to lean upon a lower rock to his left, a position which now afforded him a clear view down to the pond.

He stared off in that direction for several moments before the scene registered:

The girl was gone. So was the horse.

He began to laugh. Abruptly, he halted.

"Well . . . well, well . . ."

He turned and began to trudge back up the hillside.

". . . the hell with her."

When Baran reentered the sitting room, he found the scene changed very little. The man was still unconscious, but less pale than he had been earlier.

Semirama turned her head and smiled.

"Back so soon, Baran?"

He nodded.

"I was too late. She's gone. The horse is, too, for that matter . . ."

"Console yourself with a slave-girl."

He moved nearer.

"This fellow goes to the cellar now," he said. "You're right. We must keep him around to await the master's judgment."

"I want to be certain he is going to make it, first," she said.

At that moment, Dilvish moaned softly.

"There you are," said Baran with a smile. "He lives. A couple of you jackasses get him to his feet and follow me."

Semirama rose and stood nearer to him than she usually did.

"Really, Baran, it might be better if we wait a little longer."

He raised his right hand to the vicinity of her breasts, then suddenly snapped his fingers.

"Better for whom?" he asked. "No, my dear. He is a prisoner like all the rest. We must do our duty and store him safely away. You have shown me the light."

He turned to the two slaves who had drawn Dilvish's arms across their shoulders and raised him, head hanging, feet dragging.

"This way," he called, walking toward the door. "I'll do the honors myself."

Semirama followed.

"I'll just come along," she said, "to be sure that he makes it."

"Can't take your eyes off him, eh?"

She did not reply, but went with them out of the room and across the great hall. Her eyes wandered for a moment as she wondered again at the strange decorations and furnishings that marked it so distinctively—the mighty glass tree which hung inverted from the ceiling; the tapestries depicting young men with white hair drawn back, almost like some sort of headgear, the ladies with impossibly towering hairdos, skirts enormously billowed; elaborately carved and inlaid tables; carved chairs, all curves, upholstered only in places, colorful medallions worked into their fabrics; long mirrors; tiles of peculiar composition upon the floors; long, heavy drapes; a strange piece of furniture possessed of a keyboard, which produced musical tones when the keys were depressed.

There was something about the room which seemed unnatural even in this most unnatural of places. Occasionally, in passing through it, she had glimpsed in the depths of the mirrors reflections of

persons and things not present—fleeing, fading—
too briefly seen to be identified. And one night she
had heard a great deal of music and laughter and
babbling in a foreign tongue she could not identify,
coming from this hall. Intending either to join the
party or to blast a horde of supernatural intruders
with two extended fingers, she had made her way
down the stairs and along the corridor, had entered.
The music ceased. The room was empty. But
within the mirrors, a great crowd of beautiful and
variously dressed people stood almost frozen in
mid-movement, heads turned to regard her—and in
particular there had been a tall, almost familiar man
in some sort of pale uniform, a bright ribbon running diagonally across its breast, who had turned
away from his partner and smiled at her. For a
moment only she had hesitated, then moved to
enter the mirror and join him. The entire tableau
had vanished instantly, leaving the mirror as empty
as the hall, her arms, a sorcerer's conscience.

When she had asked Tualua about it, he did
not know or seem to care what had happened. The
castle, he had told her, writhing luxuriously in his
fetid pool, had always existed and always would
exist. It contained many strange things, and many
strange things passed through it. None of them
meant much to him.

As they departed the great hall, four notes were
somehow struck from the piece of furniture with
the keyboard, though no one was near it. Baran
paused and looked back, looked at it, looked at
her, shrugged, and passed on.

She followed them to the rear of the hall. The
unconscious man moaned again, and she reached
out and seized his wrist, satisfying herself that the
pulse there was strong.

". . . nor your hands, either," said Baran, noting the gesture.

Behind them, Melbriniononsadsazzersteldregand-ishfeltselior screamed and raced for another exit. He had seen something in a mirror which had frightened him.

They made their way to a stairwell which led down into the chamber beneath the castle. At its head, Baran trimmed a lantern and lighted it from a nearby brazier. Then, holding it aloft, he led the way down into the murky recess, apparently untroubled by his intermittent vertigo.

As they descended, their prisoner gave signs of awakening, tossing his head and seeking to obtain footing. Semirama reached forward to touch his cheek.

"It's going to be all right, Selar," she said. "It is going to be all right."

She heard Baran chuckle.

"How do you propose making good on that promise, dearie?" he asked.

Could he be faking? she wondered suddenly. Already recovered, gathering his strength, getting ready to break loose and flee through the darkness? Baran is strong and armed, and Selar does not even know where he is. And if he escapes now, Baran will set up a search that will result in his death. How to tell him to wait, to continue the ruse, to remain a prisoner for a time?

They reached the bottom of the stair, turned left. The darkness was heavy with chill, moisture-laden air. The gray stone of the wall to their left glistened and trickled in the lantern light.

The story of Corbryant and Thyseld had been popular in her day—the girl who had had to act as her lover's jailer, lest her father kill him. She wondered whether it was still current, whether

Baran would have heard of it at all. It was an Elvish tale ... Did Baran understand High Elvish—a difficult tongue, unlike any other she knew or knew of?

She reached out and took hold of Dilvish's right biceps. The arm grew tense.

"Know you the fate of Corbryant?" she asked quickly and softly in that tongue.

There was a long pause.

Then, "I do," he stated.

"So I to thee," she told him.

She felt his arm relax. She hoped that he was counting his footsteps, numbering the turns. She squeezed his arm and released it.

They passed a series of cross-corridors, down some of which rapid clicking noises and grunting sounds echoed. As they neared one, the sounds seemed to be approaching rapidly from their right. Baran raised his head and halted. He lowered the lantern.

So quickly that she was almost uncertain as to what had occurred, a horde of snouted, piglike creatures of considerable size, running on their hind legs, tore past with snuffling, panting noises. Some of them appeared to be carrying cushions and earthenware jugs. As they vanished in the distance, it seemed almost as if they had begun chanting.

"The little bastards are out in force," Baran remarked. "A few of them always manage to make it upstairs and disturb me when I'm in the library."

"They've never bothered me," she answered. "But then, I read in my room. Grotesque little things ..."

"Bet they'd make good eating. Which reminds me, my dinner is growing cold. Come along ..."

He proceeded, coming at length into a large

chamber where one torch flamed, one guttered, and two had turned to ashes in wall sockets. He took up two fresh ones from a bundle by the wall, lit them from the flaming one, hung them in the empty sockets. He headed toward the third doorless opening to the left.

"Get chains," he said.

A rack of chains with a shelf of locks stood near the pile of torches. The slave on Dilvish's left reached out and seized a set of chains as they passed. Semirama moved to his side and chose a set of locks from the shelf.

"I'll carry them," she said. "Your hands are full."

The man nodded, chains hung over his left arm, and continued. She followed, going after them all into the room where Hodgson, Derkon, Odil, Vane, Galt, and Lorman were chained to the curved walls. It seemed that there had been another . . .

Baran raised his lantern and nodded in the direction of the empty chains and gore-bespattered wall where the fat sorcerer whom the demon was now digesting had hung.

"Over there," he said. "Chain him to that ring."

The other prisoners looked on in complete silence, not stirring from the positions into which they had frozen upon Baran's entry.

The slaves half carried, half walked Dilvish to the position along the wall and threaded the chains through the massive ring fastened there, ignoring those which already hung slack along the damp stone.

"Now you'll know right where he is any time you need him," Baran remarked, "if you don't mind an audience."

She turned and looked Baran up and down, once.

"You long ago ceased to be amusing," she said. "Now I only find you vulgar—and more than a little disgusting."

She turned away and moved toward the place where the slaves were wrapping the chains about Dilvish's limbs. She passed them the locks and they secured them in place. She locked each in turn as it was positioned. Baran followed her over and tested the fastenings.

He grunted an affirmative as he checked the last. He rattled the chains as he rose, gave Semirama a sidelong look, and smiled slyly.

"Makes quite a racket," he observed. "If you come by, the whole castle will know what you're about."

Semirama covered her mouth and yawned.

"Takes your breath away, eh?"

She smiled and turned toward Dilvish.

"Is this what you wanted to see?" she said to Baran.

She embraced Dilvish and kissed him full on the mouth, pressing her entire body up against him.

As the seconds passed, Baran began to shift uneasily. The slaves looked away.

Finally, she drew away with a laugh.

"Of course, I'm passionately devoted to this stranger who has come as a trespasser to steal from us," she said. She turned suddenly and slapped Dilvish. "Insolent dog!" she announced, her face a mask of fury.

She stalked from the cell without looking back.

Baran glanced at Dilvish and grinned. Then he recovered the lantern from the ledge where he had set it and departed the room, followed by the slaves.

Outside, Semirama was pacing near the mouth of the corridor they had followed.

"I knew you'd wait for the light," Baran remarked as he approached.

She did not reply.

"You've no idea how peculiar it looked," he said when he came abreast of her.

"A kiss?" she replied with much puzzlement. "Really, Baran . . ."

"Finding you ministering to the lout the way you were," he said.

"I didn't want him to die," she answered.

"Now or later? Why not?"

"He's a curiosity . . . the first Elf to come this way. They're a peculiar people. Usually keep to themselves. Some say 'arrogant.' I thought it might amuse your master to discover this one's reasons for being here."

"And some say 'unlucky,' " Baran stated. "They can be dangerous also."

"So I've heard. Well, this one's secure."

"When I came in and saw you taking care of an interloper that way—it disturbed me, of course . . ."

"Are you trying to apologize for all of your nasty little remarks?"

Baran stalked on into the corridor, his shadow writhing in the lantern light.

"Yes," his voice came back.

"Good," she said, following him. "Not as gracious as a queen deserves, but doubtless the best I'll get from you."

Baran grunted and continued. Whether he intended to expand upon his most recent comment was never to be known, as he halted abruptly, his grunt submerged by a wave of louder ones.

He lowered the lantern and pressed back against

the wall. Semirama and the slaves did the same. The noises in the cross-corridor grew louder.

Suddenly, heading in the same direction the others had earlier, the shadowy forms of eleven of the piglike figures, tusks gleaming, went jogging past in the gloom, each clad in a long-sleeved, tunic-like garment bearing strange numerals. One carried a human skull under its left forelimb.

"My dinner must be getting cold," said Baran, raising the lantern. "Let's get out of here."

Several minutes later, they were making their way up the long stair. Near the top, a shadowy figure came into view. Baran raised the lantern.

As soon as the face became visible, Baran called out, "I thought I left you to watch the mirror. What are you doing here?"

"Another servant told me you were below, sir. The light you set me to watching—it's gone out!"

"What! So soon? I'll have to summon a replacement immediately. Very well. You're dismissed."

"Wait!" Semirama ordered.

The slave looked at her and fear came into his heart.

"Just what mirror are you talking about?" she asked as she mounted the final stairs. "Surely not that in the north room upstairs—the one in the iron frame?"

The man grew pale.

"Yes, Highness," he said, "the same."

Baran had already extinguished the lantern and set it upon a shelf. He turned toward Semirama now, smiling weakly. Semirama had suddenly drawn herself up very straight and her eyes were flashing. He was not unaware of the arcane significance of the gesture her left hand was now commencing, though he had never suspected she might contain such a force.

"Wait, Majesty! Forbear!" he cried. "It is not as you might think! Give me leave to explain!" and he wondered whether he could summon the Extra Hand before she completed the gesture.

She paused.

"Tell me, then."

He sighed.

"In attempting to solve the problem of the jammed mirror," he said, "I sent a spirit within it to investigate other astral damage. I was going to confer with it shortly to learn the extent of the troubles. I set this man to watching, in case there were any unusual developments. You have just heard his report. I should go at once and try to determine what occurred. It may give us the clue we need to open the mirror once again."

Her hand dropped.

"Yes," she said, "you had better be going. Let me know what you learn."

"I will. I will do that."

He turned and broke into a run.

Semirama looked at the two slaves who had assisted in transporting Dilvish and at the one who had just brought Baran the message.

"What are you standing here for?" she said. "Return to your duties or your quarters, as the cases may be."

They departed quickly. She watched until they were out of sight. Only then did she turn and make her way through the great hall, heading toward the doorway which led to the north-south corridor.

The hall had grown darker now that the sun was sinking, its only windows being high upon the west wall. As she passed eastward within it, she saw a slight movement off to her left. The form of a light-haired man who was not present in the hall was there in the mirror, standing beside a white pillar which was also not present in the hall. She paused and stared.

It was the man she had seen on the night of the invisible party, alone now, wearing a green robe, smiling. She had not realized on the last occasion just how handsome he was, how very much he resembled—

He raised a hand and beckoned to her. A place in the glass began to shimmer and she felt almost as if she could pass through at that point to join him.

She shrugged her shoulders and shook her head, smiling back at him. Just her luck to be in such a hurry . . .

Exiting the hall, she moved quickly along the corridor, passing an occasional servant lighting tapers in sconces and high candlesticks. She continued back into the shadow-decked heart of the place until she came to the gallery which ran along the front of the building, leading at last to the Chamber of the Pit. She paused only to look out through the window again, down to where she had first seen him.

The pond was still in clear, close view, and the girl and the horse were indeed gone. What had she been to him, anyway? Semirama wondered as she reached out to reverse the focusing spell.

The pond reflected the mountains, part of the castle, and the setting sun. The thin strip of beach beside it shone whitely, smooth; the rocks of the slope were occasional, dark interruptions.

For a moment, then, it appeared that she saw a quick movement, below and far to the right.

She hesitated, then altered the window's focus, shifting it, bringing that section of slope nearer. She studied it for several minutes, but there was no recurrence.

She smiled faintly, pleased that she had not surprised another fortune-seeker at close quarters. It
did emphasize the need for haste in her present
undertaking, however, she decided as she detuned
the glass and the prospect slid backward and away.

Departing the window, she hurried along the
gallery, sand crunching beneath her sandals. The
distinctive odor of the place came to her now.
When she entered the room, she felt the humid
warmth of the pit.

She approached it, seated herself upon the edge,
and gave voice to the call. Minutes passed, and
though she repeated it several times, there was no
response. This was not extraordinary, for he medi-
tated at times, withdrawing much of his awareness
from the world at large. She hoped that he was not
beginning one of his periodic states of dormancy,
however. It would be a piece of very bad timing
for him to undertake it now.

She uttered the call again. There were other ex-
planations also, but she did not like to think of
any of them. She leaned far forward and added a
note of urgency.

Then she felt his presence within her mind, approaching, gathering strength, indefinably troubled. She braced herself for a purely mental
communication which did not occur. Instead, the
water began to roil. She waited, but more time
passed and still he did not appear. Waves of feelings then began to wash over her—dark, malevolent
things rising batlike from the pit—touched only
lightly and occasionally with the qualities of play-
fulness and curiosity which normally dominated
this place.

"What is the matter?" she inquired in that chirping tongue she used here.

Again there was no reply, but the waves of

feelings, emotions, increased. The atmosphere of the place grew somber, sinister. Then suddenly it broke, and an almost cheerful sensation tinged with a note of triumph arose. This grew in force as the others were swept away, pushed into the background. The waters were disturbed again, and a portion of that amorphous, dark form broke the surface, a vague, pearly aura glowing faintly about it, blurring patterns shifting constantly within it, distorting the shifting bulk beneath them.

"Sister and lover and priestess, greetings, from the many places where I dwell," rose the formal salutation in that same language.

"And to you, from that one in this place, Tualua, kin of the Elders. You are troubled. What is the cause? Tell me."

"Queen in this place, Semirama, it is the painful growth cycle of those of my kind. Kin to both darkness and light, I possess both natures."

"As do we, Tualua."

"Ah, but men manage to mix them in the brief span of their days. It must make life so much simpler."

"It brings its problems."

"Ah, but ours brings eon after eon of recrimination, each time for the previous cycle when the opposite ruled—until that hoped-for, impossible day when our natures merge and we are fit to join our kin in the places beyond this hell of polarities."

An almost unbearable wave of sadness swept over her, and she wept uncontrollably. A tentacle rose, almost shyly, and its tip touched her foot.

"Do not grieve for me, child. Weep rather for mankind. For when the dark will comes over me and I repent these days, my power will go forth across the land and all men will suffer—save yourself, as you serve me, for you shall grow strong and bright and hard and cold as the morning star—and I shall be stronger than ever before and the world will tremble onto its foundations as in the early days when others of my kind of disjunct cycle warred for the soul of man."

"Is there nothing that can be done?" she asked.

"I can still hold it back, and I will for as long as I can."

"What of the good mage Jelerak and the debt all of your kind owe to him of old?"

"What debt there was, Semirama, has long since been paid, believe me. Nor is he that same man whom once you knew."

"What do you mean?"

"He is—changed. Perhaps he, too, has his light and dark natures."

"I find this difficult to believe, though I have recently heard rumors. The last I knew of him in the old days, he had been ill for a long while—years, possibly—following the fall of Hohorga . . ."

"Then it may be kindest to say that he never recovered."

"He treated me very kindly when he called me back . . ."

"Of course. He needed you. You possess an extremely specialized skill—for a human. And there is something else . . .

"I regret most," he continued, "that he and I may soon have much in common."

"You have just turned my world upside down," she said.

"I am sorry, but I had no way of foreseeing when the change would begin to come over me. I will still help you with anything you wish, in any way that I can, for as long as I am able."

She reached out and touched the tentacle.

"If there is any way that I can help you . . ."

"Nothing," he said. "No mortal can help me. Ironically, I will become truly mad for a time, during the transition period. I will send you away before it comes over me, to a place I have provided for you beyond time and space, where you will know much joy. My other self will doubtless recall you when there is need for your services."

"It saddens me greatly to hear these things."

"And me to tell them. So let us talk instead of what it was that brought you here just now."

"That matter has just been further confused," she said, "by things you have told me. Baran is doing something to the mirror. He's placed at least one spirit inside it. He's probably installing another right now—"

"I have paid small heed to these mortal affairs, save as you bade me. So tell me now who Baran is and why anything he might do with a mirror should matter to you."

"Baran is the dark, heavy man who sometimes accompanies me here."

"The one with the hand trick?"

"Yes. He is Jelerak's steward in this place. The mirror—in a chamber partway up the north tower —is a means of transportation for Jelerak among his many abodes. Jelerak was injured in a sorcerer's duel some time ago, and we thought that he might be coming here, where I could beg power of you to heal him. While we awaited his arrival, many others who thought him dead or weakened sought to storm this place, that they might attempt to bind you to their own uses."

A ripple of amusement flowed past her.

"It was then that I thought of the reason for which Jelerak had restored me—to assist you during last summer's illness . . ."

"My first spell of madness in centuries. Up until

then I had been furnishing him whatever power he asked of me for those favors of long ago of which you spoke. He did not realize what was occurring. Neither did I at the time."

"Nor I, of course. Though I might have recalled some very old dark sayings, I had never witnessed the condition before. But when the interlopers came, I thought it well to suggest you repeat the effects upon the land hereabout in full awareness, to keep them away. I knew that this could not impede Jelerak, for he could always employ the mirror to journey here. I would have told Baran my strategy, but by then I was finding his attentions annoying. Better to let him believe that a more difficult situation such as last summer's had arisen, and that I was the only one who might deal with it effectively. The deception gave me more power over him. But all this while, I believed the mirror to be in proper condition. Now I am not so certain. I believe that he might have been blocking it all along."

"Why would he do such a thing?"

"When you set the land without in turmoil, it barred every easy means of entry here, save for the mirror. If he found a way to block the mirror, then we were completely isolated, and Jelerak himself could not return for the renewal he would be seeking. The purpose, I believe now, is that Baran has become like the invaders themselves. He wished to keep this place to himself while he sought after a means of controlling you."

"He does not then realize that I served Jelerak willingly, not under any compulsion—as the doings of humans have meant little to me these many years?"

"No. I never told him. The less he knew, the better."

"Then what is the problem?"

"Now I am uncertain. Originally, I came to ask you to open the way of the mirror and to keep it open against any attempts he may make to close it off again. This, so that Jelerak might return and be refreshed and deal with Baran as he sees fit. Now, though, that you have told me what you have about Jelerak, I do not know what to say."

"It would be a simple matter to unblock the mirror, though I could not promise to hold it open were another spell of madness to come over me."

". . . and then I was going to ask you to recommence the emanations and disturb the land again, to keep unwanted visitors out while giving Jelerak opportunity to enter through the glass—also to convince Baran that you were still uncontrollable, so that he would not bother me to be his accomplice in a fruitless task."

"And now?"

"Now it has become a choice between evils. I do not know. Baran is not nearly so wise, and he likes me. I believe that he would be easy for me to control. Yet I still feel a measure of loyalty to Jelerak. No matter what you may say of him, he has always treated me well."

"No matter what the situation, you might depend upon that."

"Out of respect to my station, of course. He was no stranger to the court of Jandar."

"That may or may not be true, but it was something more personal that I had in mind."

She stiffened. Then she laughed.

"No, that I cannot believe. Jelerak? He was always almost monkish in his habits. He was devoted solely to his Arts."

"He could have called back any of your illustrious line to talk with me."

"True."

"His main love is power and the domination of men's spirits. Yet there are two human attachments of which he has not entirely rid himself—a small, fraternal feeling toward the priests of Babrigore, and a measure of devotion toward yourself. You were always the unattainable queen and priestess."

"Then he hid it well."

"But not from Tualua, for I have seen his heart and all things in it—even those of which he himself is unaware. But I tell you this now for a reason. My will is crumbling, and I wish to provide for my own before it is completely shattered. Even as we have been speaking here I cast my eye along future time-lines. There is a dark spot ahead which I cannot penetrate. I believe that he is in some way involved beyond that point. My first intent was to send you to the place I have prepared for you, for your protection."

Her thoughts ran back to the man in chains.

"I will not go," she stated.

"I saw that also. Which is why I have told you of the sorcerer's human frailty regarding yourself. It is a slim thing at best, of which even he is only partly aware and does not fully understand. I caution you not to rely upon it, yet the knowledge may serve you in some way during the dark hour."

She embraced the tentacle.

"Tualua! Tualua! Perhaps you are stronger than you think. Can you not fight the dark will and perhaps overcome it?"

The atmosphere about her became heavy and brooding even as she spoke.

"That," Tualua finally answered, "is not the pattern of my kind, as I understand it. I am trying and I will continue to try. Yet I fear that my struggles only train it to greater strength."

"Do not give up. Hold out for as long as you can. Call upon your kin the Elder Gods if you must!"

Something like laughter shook the vault.

"My illustrious forbears have long since abandoned this plane to which I am confined. They would not hear me in their high abodes. No, we must prepare ourselves for a trial, and I must concern myself again with human matters, for I find them entwined with my own. Listen now to what I say, for I feel the madness rising again . . ."

The steaming water of his brightly tiled pool covered Holrun's body to just above shoulder level, and the aroma of an exotic incense filled the air around him. The planes of his face were angular; his eyes—now half lidded—were dark and given to dartings inquisitive and expressive. His mouth, even in repose, quirked toward a slightly sinister smile. He was leaning forward now as one of his favorites, kneeling behind him, massaged his shoulders beneath water level. Another passed him a cooling drink in the carved, curved tusk of an extinct predator. He sipped from it and handed it back, trailing his fingertips along the girl's arm as she withdrew.

When his crystal summoned him, he cursed softly and ran a hand through his thatch of unruly brown hair, shrugging off the other girl's ministrations, and turned toward the large globe he had set within the wall surrounded by a mosaic of delicate tiles in the form of an enormous eye. He focused his attention and the image of Meliash appeared within the pupil.

"I am sorry to disturb you," Meliash began.

"It happens, when you're the youngest member of the Council. Good thing, too, I suppose, if you want to get anything done. Those doddering old unwrapped mummies would take forever to decide to relieve themselves. Someone has to goose them with a hot poker every now and then, and I'm elected. How's everything in the Sangaris? I—"

"The Kannais."

"Yeah, the Kannais. I really envy you being out in the field, you know? This administrative stuff —well, it's got to be done."

He halted abruptly and stared, beginning to smile.

"Yes," Meliash said. "There have been some changes here recently, and I feel that the Council ought to be made aware of them. We've turned up some very interesting information, also. In fact, I believe that the time has finally come for the Council to take action in a matter directly involving Jel—"

"Easy! Easy!" Holrun was suddenly standing, palm upraised, as his masseuse rushed to fit a robe over his shoulders. "The ether has ears as well as other appendages, I sometimes think. Let me take this on my other crystal. It's got security spells you wouldn't believe. I'll call you right back."

He waved his hand and Meliash faded.

Holrun stalked out of the pool and stepped into a pair of sandals. He headed away from the grotto and down a sloping tunnel, raising two fingers to his mouth and whistling a loud, shrill note. A pale light began to glow within long bands of white stone set into the tunnel walls at either hand.

Smiling, he turned a corner and entered an L-shaped chamber carved out of stone on two levels. He snapped his fingers and logs began blazing within a recess directly ahead, the smoke rising up a jagged fissure screened by orange stalactites about which long chains of carved bodies transmitted erotic impulses in great spirals; fat candles flickered to life on high stands, revealing a neat but densely packed room containing almost every variety of magical equipment employed by over thirty nations and tribes; every visible spot on the floor, vaulted ceiling and barrel walls was painted with arcane symbols.

He moved immediately to a shelf at his left and took down a small lemon-wood casket which he bore to a stand in a corner near the fire. With his foot, he drew a low stool covered with gray fur across the geometrically patterned rug. Opening the casket, he withdrew a smoky, almost black crystal which he set in place upon the stand. Then he seated himself upon the stool, took a single deep breath and released it, said one word:

"Meliash!"

The crystal cleared only slightly and the form of Meliash appeared dimly within it.

"How's that?" he said to him.

"You sound so far away," came the minuscule piping reply.

"Can't be helped. The protective spells are pressing all around us, like creditors at a funeral. But you can talk freely. What is all this about wanting the Council to do something to Jelerak?"

"I believe he passed this way in disguise just this morning, and that he's trying to get into the castle now."

"Well, shit, man! It *is* his place. If going home is the worst thing he's up to these days, I don't see where—"

"You don't understand. He is weaker now than at any time within living memory. I am certain that he is trying to get in there to tap one of his major sources of power, to renew himself. And the possibility of his being able to is not all that good—not if Tualua has entered one of the periodic fits of madness his kind are liable to. And I believe this to be the case. Further—"

Holrun waved his hand.

"Wait. All of this is very interesting, but I don't understand what you're getting at. Even weakened, he would be a formidable foe. There have been all sorts of secret studies and auguries on the results of possible clashes with him."

"You know what those are worth," Meliash said. "Sooner or later the man will destroy or subvert the entire organization, as he has so many individual members. I know that he has a whole bloc of followers among us, and so do you. Sooner or later we are going to have to deal with him, and I think this is the most favorable opportunity we've ever had. I've heard you say yourself that you wanted it to occur during your lifetime."

"Look, I don't deny it. But that was informally and off the record. The Council is a conservative bunch. That's why they've had this hands-off policy on him for years."

"There is more," Meliash stated.

"Let's have it."

"A man went in there this morning with the express intention of killing Jelerak."

Holrun snorted.

"That's all?" he asked. "Do you know how many have tried? How few have even come close? No, that's not worth much one way or the other."

"His name was Dilvish and he rode a metal horse. I've just recently learned who he is."

"Dilvish the Damned? He's there? You're sure? Part Elf? Tall? Light? Wears the green boots?"

"Yes. And he was once a Society member—"

"I know, I know! Dilvish! Gods! I'd hate to

see him die this close to his goal. He was one of my boyhood heroes—the Colonel of the East. And when he came back from Hell . . . He may get him, you know? If I had to choose the assassin myself, I wouldn't look any further. Dilvish . . ."

"So I was thinking, if the Society wanted to avoid a direct confrontation, perhaps they could simply find a way to help the man and stay out of the picture themselves."

Holrun was not looking at him. He was staring off into space.

"What do you think?" Meliash asked.

"Tell me about that place. What's it like?"

"The disturbances have ceased. The land is quiet about it now. I can see the castle in the distance. Lights have been lit within it. There may be a map of the interior in the archives. I should have checked with Rawk. Jelerak's steward in the place is Baran of Blackwold, a middling good sorcerer—"

"Isn't there something peculiar about the place itself? Most old castles have histories."

"This one fades back into legend. It is reputed to be the oldest building in the world, predating the human race. It is said to be haunted up to the hilt. There is also supposed to be some connection with the Elder Gods."

"One of those, eh? All right, listen. You've gotten me interested. Keep everything to yourself and don't do anything foolish. I am going to take this up with the Council in emergency session immediately. I am going to try selling them on a change in policy. But don't get your hopes up. Most of them wouldn't recognize an opportunity if it came up and bit them on the ass. I'll get back to you as soon as I have something, though, and we can decide what to do next."

He broke the connection, rose, stared for a moment into the fire, smiled, and crossed the chamber.

"Hot damn!"

He snapped his fingers and the lights went out.

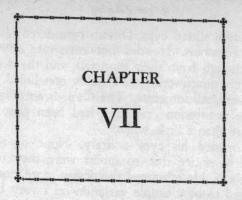

CHAPTER

VII

Dilvish heard their laughter, their jests. "Kiss of death" figured prominently among them. But, oblivious to most of it, he hung trembling, his thoughts a chaos of revived memories. His head had ceased hurting. Whatever the woman had done to it had worked with amazing swiftness. The pain he felt now was a mental thing, brought on by the violent touch of a demon. For a time, he was back again in the Houses of Pain, and memories he had sealed off spilled forth like lava, burning him.

After a time, he thought of where he was and why he was there, and a hate stronger than pain took hold. He attempted to refocus his attention, succeeded. Their words came to him:

". . . get the demon-catcher repaired. They rubbed a lot of it out when they dragged him in."

"Can you reach his part? He won't be any help for awhile."

"Maybe."

"Odil, you'll have to stretch again."

Through slitted eyes, Dilvish considered his six fellow prisoners. He did not recognize any of them, though from their shop talk and the design they were constructing, he quickly concluded that they were all sorcerers. Their appearances gave him the impression that they had been prisoners for more than a little while.

He opened his eyes entirely. None of them seemed to notice this, so intent were they upon their labors. He examined the design more closely. It proved to be a simple variation on a very basic pattern learned by most apprentices in their first year. Impulsively, he extended a green-booted toe and completed the portion nearest him.

"Look! Lover Boy's come around!" one of them called. Then, as heads began to turn, "I'm Galt, and this is Vane," he said.

As Dilvish nodded, the others spoke:

". . . Hodgson."

". . . Derkon"—to his left.

". . . Lorman"—to his right.

". . . Odil."

"And I am Dilvish," he told them.

Derkon's head jerked in his direction again and his eyes met those of Dilvish.

"Colonel Dilvish? You were at Portaroy?" he asked.

"The same."

"I was there."

"I'm afraid I don't recall . . ."

Derkon laughed.

"I was on the other side—Sorcerer's Corps—casting strong spells for your failure. You were so ungracious as to win, anyway. Cost me my commission."

"I can't really say I'm sorry about that. Why are you drawing demon-traps all over the floor?"

"They think the damned place is a pantry. They wander in occasionally and eat us."

"Good reason, then. Are you all in for the same thing?"

"Yes," said Derkon.

"No," said Hodgson.

Dilvish raised an eyebrow.

"He's just making a metaphysical point," Derkon explained.

"A moral one," Hodgson corrected. "We wanted the power in this place for different reasons."

"But we all wanted it," Derkon said, smiling. "We were all good enough or lucky enough to get through to the castle, and here it ended." He gestured, rattling his chains dramatically. "My spells went wild and I faced Baran man to man. He sneaked up on me with his extra hand, though."

"Extra hand?"

"Yes. He grew himself a spare appendage on another plane. Brings it through whenever he needs it. If you ever get out of here and run into him, remember that it can be quicker than the eye."

"I will."

"Where is your metal steed?"

Dilvish looked pensive.

"Alas. He suffers the fate I once did. He is become a statue." He gestured vaguely with his head. "Out there."

Hodgson cleared his throat.

"Have you a preference for either extreme within the Art?" he inquired.

"My interest in the Art recently has been minimal—and practical rather than technical," he replied.

Hodgson chuckled.

"Then may I inquire as to what ends you would

employ the Old One's power, should you achieve control of it?"

"I did not come seeking power," Dilvish said.

"What, then?" Lorman asked him.

"Just Jelerak in the flesh—and a few minutes to terminate his relationship with it."

There were gasps from around the room.

"Really?" Derkon said.

Dilvish nodded.

"Brave, foolish, or both—there is something attractive about an outrageous and futile undertaking. I applaud you. It is unfortunate you'll never have the opportunity to try."

"That remains to be seen," Dilvish said.

"But tell me," Hodgson persisted, "where your greatest strength in the Art lies. You must meet strong magic with something other than a scowl and a sword. What is the color of your main power?"

Dilvish thought upon the Awful Sayings, of which probably he alone on earth knew all.

"Black as the Pit from which it comes, I'm afraid," he told him.

Derkon and Lorman chuckled as he said it.

"That gives us three out of seven, with a couple of grays," Derkon said. "Not bad."

"I don't really think of myself as a sorcerer," Dilvish said.

This time all of them laughed.

"It's like being a little bit dead or pregnant, eh?"

"Who raised the legions of Shoredan?"

"Where did you get that metal horse?"

"How did you make it to the castle?"

"Aren't elfboots magic?"

"Thanks for your help on the demon-trap."

Dilvish looked puzzled.

"I never thought of it all that way," he said. "Perhaps there is some truth in what you say . . ."

They laughed again.

"You are indeed peculiar," Derkon finally said. "But, of course, what other way is there to fight black magic than with more of the same?"

"White magic!" said Hodgson.

The grays only laughed at both of them.

"I'd prefer using natural weapons, if at all possible."

This time all of them laughed.

"Against him?"

"You'd never get near enough."

"Preference must be sacrificed to expedience."

"As a fly to a stallion . . ."

"A drop of water in the great desert . . ."

". . . he would dispatch you."

"Perhaps," said Dilvish, "and perhaps not."

"At least," said Derkon, "you have given us the first merriment since our capture. And, like most of our discussions, this one, also, will doubtless remain academic."

"Then let us continue in that vein," Dilvish said. "What do you plan to do if you get out of here?"

"What makes you think there is a plan?" Galt asked.

"Hush!" Vane told him.

"In every prison I have occupied, there has always been a plan," Dilvish said.

"How do we know that you are not Jelerak in disguise, playing some game with us?"

"Half a dozen sorcerers in here, of all hues, and you can't tell whether a man is under a transformation spell?"

"Our spells are no good in this place—and for that matter, there are simpler disguises than the magical sort."

"Peace!" Derkon cried. "This man is not Jelerak."

"How do you know that?" Odil asked.

"Because I have met Jelerak, and no mundane disguise could change him so. As for a magical one— There are certain things that are not changed. I am a sensitive as well as a sorcerer, and I like this man. I never liked Jelerak."

"You base it on a feeling?"

"A sensitive trusts his feelings."

"Jelerak is a fellow practitioner of Black Art," Hodgson said. "Yet you did not like him?"

"Do all scribes like one another? All soldiers? All priests? Do you like all of the white practitioners? It is like anything else. I respect his talents and some of his accomplishments, but he disturbs me personally."

"In what way?"

"I had never before met a man who I believe loved evil for its own sake."

"A strange thing for one such as yourself to condemn."

"For me the Art is a means, not an end. I am my own man."

"Yet will it tarnish you."

"Then that is my problem. Dilvish asked a question. Is anyone going to answer it?"

"I will," Hodgson said. "No, there is no real plan as such for getting us out of here. But if we should manage it, we share an intention. We mean to go to an unaffected area and there pool our powers into the channeling of Tualua's emanations, to break the maintenance spell upon this place. You are welcome to join in the effort."

"What will its results be?" Dilvish asked.

"We do not know for certain. It may be that

the place will fall apart, permitting us to escape amid the disorder."

"Stones piled upon stones tend to maintain themselves so," Dilvish said. "More likely, the place will merely be freed to age naturally. I will decline your invitation, for I must be about other matters as soon as I leave here."

Galt snorted.

"And this will be soon, I suppose?" he asked.

"Yes. But first I must know whether any of you have seen Jelerak. Is he here? Where does he keep his quarters?"

There were no replies. Dilvish looked around the room, and one by one, the men shook their heads.

"If he were here," Odil stated, "we would all be dead by now, or worse."

"As for his quarters," Galt said, "our knowledge of this place is somewhat circumscribed."

"Who was that woman," Dilvish asked, "who helped bring me here?"

The laughter began again.

"And you don't even know her?" Vane inquired.

"She is Queen Semirama of ancient Jandar," Hodgson told him, "summoned back from the dust by Jelerak himself to serve him here."

"I have heard ballads and stories of her beauty, her guile . . ." Dilvish said. "It is hard to believe she is actually here, alive, by that man's power. An ancestor of mine was said to have been one of her lovers."

"Who might that be?" Hodgson asked.

"Selar himself."

At that moment, Lorman began to wail and rattle his chains.

"Alas! Alas! It begins again, and I did not know

it had ended! We are doubly doomed—to have had such a chance and let it go by! Alas!"

"What—what is the matter?" Hodgson asked him.

"We are failed! Ruined! It would have been so easy!"

"What? What?"

But the ancient sorcerer only wailed again, then fell to cursing. A cloud materialized in the high, shadowy spaces above them and a pale blue snow began to fall from it.

"Does anyone know what he is talking about?"

They all shook their heads.

Lorman raised a bony finger, indicating the unnatural blizzard.

"That! That!" he cried. "It has only just begun again! I felt the emanations beginning. They had stopped for some time and we paid it no heed! Our magic would have worked during that time! We could have been out of here!"

He began gnashing what remained of his teeth.

A door of the sitting room off the main hall opened slowly onto the twilit world. A massive head covered with black curly hair ducked beneath the upper frame, and a heavily muscled giant of a man entered the room. Naked to the waist, he wore a short blue and black kirtle, cinched with a wide strap of leather from which an enormous scabbard descended. He turned his head slowly and raised it, nostrils twitching. Soundlessly, on buskined feet, he moved first to the mud-streaked couch, then to the far corner of the room. His eyes were an almost incandescent blue; his full beard was as curly as the rest of his hair.

He crossed to the door at his right and pushed it slowly ajar. He looked out into the main hall.

The inverted glass tree on the ceiling was burning with a light that was not fire. The floors shone slick as the surface of a pond. From somewhere near came a ticking sound. The walls of mirrors shuffled infinities as he sniffed at the stale air and stepped forward. There was no one else within the place.

As he advanced, a single chiming note sounded off to his left. He moved with great speed for one of his size, turning, striding, half drawing the blade from his scabbard.

The chime was repeated, somewhere within a tall, narrow box which stood upright within a niche to the right of the door through which he had just passed. It bore a circular face near its higher end, inscribed about with a dozen numerals; two arrows pointed in opposing directions across it. The chiming continued, and he drew nearer, studying what was visible of the mechanism within through a decorated panel of glass, counting the strokes, a smile beginning on his large mouth. It sounded seven times before it ceased, and he realized that it was the source of the ticking. He noted then that the smaller arrow was pointed at the seventh numeral. He considered the images of the sun and the moon in all its phases inscribed and painted upon its face. Suddenly, he comprehended its function and suppressed a laugh of delight at its simplicity, its elegance. He slid his blade silently to rest and turned away.

The hall had changed, or was it only the lighting? It seemed dimmer now, more threatening, and he felt as if unseen eyes watched his progress across the polished floor. The scent he had first caught in the sitting room was still mingled with another which disturbed him greatly.

The huge overhead light crackled and flickered

as he passed beneath it. Shadows darted around him and within the mirrors . . .

The mirrors. He passed a large, hairy hand before his eyes. For but a moment it seemed that the mirror to his right showed something which did not share the hall with him—a large, strangely shaped patch of darkness. It was no longer evident, but as he advanced he kept his eyes upon the place where it might have been.

Of the scents he followed, the wrong one was growing stronger . . .

The entire castle seemed to shudder, once, lightly, about him . . .

The light fixture swayed, and the shadows danced again . . .

Abruptly, within an odd little piece of furniture at the farther side of the hall, music began . . .

The blackness was back, half hidden behind a pillar which hid nothing on this side of the glass . . .

He moved doggedly ahead now, ignoring everything but the scents.

(Had the tapestry near the corner ahead, to the right, just stirred slightly?)

The black thing slid out from behind a mirrored pillar, and he halted, staring at it.

It was a huge, horselike beast fashioned of metal that pranced forward, tossed its head, and regarded him. It almost seemed to be laughing at him.

He stared, and bewilderment mingled with disbelief upon his countenance as it seemed to be walking straight toward him. Then it turned abruptly and mimicked his advance into the hall, even pausing to inspect the image of the clock within its niche. When it came abreast of him, it halted and turned to return his gaze.

Suddenly its eyes flickered and glowed, and a wisp of smoke rose from its nostrils.

It lowered its head and leaned forward. A rush of flames emerged from its mouth, spreading about the hall, filling the entire wall of mirrors.

The man raised his hand and turned away.

The mirrors upon the opposite wall also contained the conflagration. The brightness became intense. Yet there was no heat, no sound . . .

The black beast had disappeared behind the wall of flame, yet the man had the strange feeling that the glass could crack at any moment and the metal thing emerge, charging toward him.

There was an oppressive feeling of ancient magic all about. Whether it emanated from the Old One somewhere within or was a part of the very structure of the castle itself, he could not tell.

Dragging his gaze from the wall, he began to move forward again. The tapestry was stirring once more. It was obvious now that there was a large form hidden behind it. He headed directly toward it.

Before he reached it, however, it was whipped aside and the mismatched eyes of a demon regarded him.

"The flames made me think I was being sent home," he muttered. "But here is only a mortal man—not even one of those I may not harm."

His long, forked tongue emerged to lick his lips.

"Dinner!" he concluded.

The man halted and his hands moved to his belt.

"You are mistaken," said the man in the same language, "Melbriniononsadsazzersteldregandishfeltselior. And the flames were already banked on the day of your spawning."

"How is it, kin of the apes, that you know my name when I do not know you?"

"You are mistaken," the man repeated, "for you

will be sent home. And before you go I will whisper the answer to your final question, and you will know me."

He unfastened his belt and lowered it, with the heavy blade and scabbard, to the floor.

The music grew wilder and the flames continued their dance as the demon came toward him. He moved to meet him, a grim smile upon his lips.

"Presumption, thy name is man," said the demon as he sprang upon him.

"You are mistaken," answered the other as he avoided the snapping fangs, blocked the slashing talons and seized hold of him.

Quickly, they were knotted into a complex array of limbs and they fell to the floor and began rolling. Eyes seemed to open within the flames, to regard them.

Holrun had hung the mirror upon a section of bare wall between a desk and the hearth, covering over threescore and eight interesting runes and symbols. Now he reclined himself upon a heap of cushions before it, drawing upon his water pipe as he considered the approach, slowing his heartbeat, tensing and relaxing groups of muscles. After a time, he set the mouthpiece aside, still thinking of the thing he had learned at the Council meeting, where they had hovered disembodied above the Kannais, considering the Castle Timeless. Jelerak employed a system of mirrors to transport himself between his strongholds. It would require access to one of the mirrors and a full knowledge of the governing spell to utilize the system as he did. The castle itself was surrounded by a hard, dark aura which completely shielded it against psychic penetration. It was too far away for immediate physical access, and the land about it might begin its mad dance again at any time, anyway. Holrun had committed the appearance and the feeling of the place to memory. Upon returning to his body and his quarters, he had checked in his voluminous library for any reference he could think of which might bear upon the subject of the mirrors.

Now he released his spirit once more, to return to that place. Soon the Castle Timeless winked below him, immense and sinister. Its psychic shield still held, but there were places beyond places—planes where reality was reduced to a simple vision . . .

He shifted to that of pure energy and found his way barred there, too. Then an archetypal place of pure forms, where he was also excluded. With considerably more effort than he had thus far employed, he moved to the plane of essences.

Ah . . .

The entire pattern of the castle was bizarre, one of the strangest things he had ever beheld. But he wasted no time cataloging wonders. Having already set his will upon locating the mirror, it stood out quite clearly for his inspection in what, in the mundane world, would be the north tower.

He approached it cautiously, searching out unusual essences in its vicinity.

There was a single man present, and from this plane the essence of an extra hand was visible. So that was Baran. Well, well . . .

He saw the spell and shifted to the plane of structures, where he felt more comfortable. It became a series of interconnected lines of various colors, all of them pulsing, beads of energy passing in seeming-random fashion from junction to junction.

Interesting. Something else was studying it also, from closer up, over on the energy plane.

He withdrew somewhat and watched the

watcher. If it could locate the starting point for him, a lot of time and energy—not to mention risk —might be saved. He did not like that fuzzy blue coiled thing in one small corner. Upon careful inspection, it seemed to be touching yet unattached . . .

His fellow student of the spell, upon closer inspection, appeared to be one of those vague, cislunar elementals normally of amorphous, fiery aspect when drawn to his own plane. Here it was an inquiring hook, pulsing redly. It traced the periphery of the spell several times, rapidly, without coming into contact with that cage of lines. It did seem to slow its passage at one sharp corner each time that it went by, however.

Each line that he beheld represented a single unit of the spell, spoken or gestured. That power which filled it was, of course, entered by Jelerak himself in accompaniment to the ritual, drawn either from his own being or from a sacrificial source. The problem for Holrun was to determine the sequence in which the structure had been created back on his own plane—a difficult task, for the beginning was not readily visible, as it would be in the work of a neophyte or even that of a journeyman with no great passion for secrecy. It was an exceedingly intricate piece of work, and Holrun felt an unwilling admiration for the man's technical proficiency.

The hook slowed at another place—a lower angle, as if suddenly attracted to something there —then passed on and paused again at the sharp corner. Holrun maintained his passive screen. He could get out now even if the spell were employed before him. It would be later that things would become dangerous. Better to let the elemental risk these preliminaries.

It slowed again at the angle, almost halting, and Holrun focused his full attention upon that place.

Yes. During the ebb of one of the pulsations he was certain that he had detected the web-thin line of an unnatural juncture where a microwedge of perception might be driven. The elemental did not seem to note it, however, and returned to the sharp corner, where it halted.

He watched, certain what would follow.

The hook extended its sharper end, making contact, applying psychic pressures at that point. The cold blue guardian sprang like an uncoiled spring into the adjacent angle. The hook struggled to free itself, then grew still. It began to shrink and moments later was completely absorbed.

The blue coil fell away and was still, pulsing more brightly now. After several more beats, it attached itself to another angle, and the additional brightness it had gained was drained out of it into the structure of the spell itself. It rolled away then and was still once more, a fuzzy blue thing.

Holrun drew nearer. He could see now that the elemental had been blocking the spell as well as studying it. Features he had at first taken as part of the construct began to flicker and fade—wedges set between open areas which must close when the spell was called upon to function. As he observed their passing, he considered the person who must have introduced the elemental into the picture in the first place. Once he became aware that it had vanished, it would take him a time to set up the conditions to summon another, should he wish to continue the study and the blockage immediately, and additional time to charge one with its task. Which should leave Holrun sufficient time to do what needed to be done without interruption.

Unless, of course, someone employed the spell

while he was about it, in which case he would be destroyed.

He advanced upon the lower angle. The only thing remaining to be determined was the direction in which the spell flowed. He had two choices. The wrong one would undo it, totally deactivating the mirror as he ran through it backward.

One line was thinner than the other, indicating a high pitch to the sorcerer's voice as he had uttered that sound. Normally, a spell commenced on a lower note than it ended, though this was not always the case. Either line, for that matter, could also represent a preliminary gesture. He moved nearer and made momentary contact with the heavier line.

The blue coil flashed toward him, but he had already withdrawn by the time it arrived, bearing one piece of information away with him: the line echoed on contact! Therefore, it was a word, not a gesture.

He watched and waited for the coil to subside. It was not so quick to settle back this time, but drifted off, exploring the larger angles.

Once he entered the spell proper, from either end, he would be safe from its attentions, which had to be put in abeyance during the structure's actual operation. The only danger then would be if the spell were employed while he was tracing it.

The coil subsided once again, and he sounded the thinner line, withdrawing instantly.

The cold blue thing acted in a predictable fashion, and he ignored it while digesting the additional information he had gained: there had been another echo; therefore, it began and ended with a word.

There was still no way of telling for certain which arm of the angle represented the beginning and which the end—save for the lower-note presumption. He retreated and regarded the spell as a whole once more, attempting to gain an overall impression of its pattern. He rummaged his memory for analogies, brooded upon them, decided that ultimately he must place his trust upon a totally subjective feeling which had been growing within him.

He rushed forward and penetrated the end of the thinner line. The striking of the cold blue thing was beyond his perception, for he was already moving within the system of the spell by the time it arrived.

He realized that he had guessed correctly as he heard the first word—a fairly standard opening—ringing all about him. He advanced through the spell, receiving impressions of each gesture, living within each word, burning them all into his memory. When he came to the end, he jumped the gap and commenced a second circuit. This time he fled through it for a total impression, rather than for a rehearsal of particulars. Again . . .

He marveled at the cunning manner in which it had been contrived, knowing full well that he would one day require a set of similar transportation devices himself. You just didn't see that sort of spellmanship these days . . .

Again.

Now it was with a more critical eye that he ran through it, seeking precisely the right point of attack . . .

Aha!

The seventh term ended with a hard consonant and the eighth began with one. The same applied to the twenty-third and twenty-fourth words. He ran by them again. The caesura between the seven-eight pair was slightly longer.

He halted and inserted a soft "t" into the gap

the next time around. Even if Jelerak were to audit his own spell, it would not be detectable between a pair of consonants. Then he spun off from his special element, creating a simple subspell system, all of whose lines paralleled and were superimposed upon existing spell-elements. When he had finished, he ran through the spell proper once again, deleting nothing. Another time around and he activated the "t" and dropped through into his own system. Perfect. The subspell actually utilized the heart of Jelerak's own system, but the linkage should be—

He trickled energy from his own being through his system, activating it, and mentally thumbed his nose at the cold blue thing as the entire construct vanished and he found himself within his own mirror, regarding his reclining form.

He departed the mirror, lowered his vibration rate, and opened his eyes. He stretched and smiled. He had done it, and he had left no footprints.

Rising, he stretched again and massaged his forehead and temples, rubbed his eyes. He began yawning as he obtained the black crystal and set it up. But he gathered his forces, focused his attention, and spoke Meliash's name.

The image appeared.

"Hi," he said. "How are they hanging?"

"Holrun! What's happened? It's been so long!"

"I've been working on this damned thing. Let me tell you about Jelerak's mirror—"

"His transport mirror?"

"The same. I just trapdoored the spell on the one in the castle."

" 'Trapdoored'?"

"Right. If that damned elemental is not in the way, it will work just as he wants it to, as often as he likes, without his ever being aware that

now have access to the spell, the mirror, the castle
—at will."

"I've never heard of such a thing."

"It's a sneaky technique I developed myself."

"What are you going to do with it?"

Holrun yawned.

"I'll know when I wake up. Right now I've got
to soak and take a nap. I'm dead."

"But this must mean you persuaded the Council
to do something."

"Come on, Meliash! You know better than that.
All I got out of them—accidentally, at that—was
the knowledge that there were such things as the
mirrors. They wouldn't touch Jelerak with a hawk-
ing gauntlet."

"Then who authorized you to trapdoor the
spell?"

"Nobody. I did it on my own."

"Won't you get in trouble if they find out?"

"Not as a private citizen. I resigned from the
Council in protest at the end of the meeting."

"I—I'm sorry."

"Oh, it wasn't the first time. Look, I've got to
get some rest before I do anything else. Bye-bye."

He blanked the crystal, cased it, and walked to
the door. He snapped his fingers as he departed
and did not look back.

At first, Semirama ignored the knocking at her
door. But when it was repeated and Lisha still did
not appear to answer it, she rose from her mound
of furs and cushions and crossed the chamber.

"Yes?"

Seeing no one when she cracked the door, she
opened it wide.

The hall was empty.

She closed the door and returned to her nest of

softness and incense, old wine and memory. The air seemed to sparkle for a moment, and tapestries and draperies fluttered as if a breeze were passing through the closed room.

"My Lady Semirama, Queen. I am here."

She looked about, saw no one.

"Here."

A dark-haired man in yellow tunic and fur leggings was staring off to her right near the foot of the bed, head lowered. He raised his head and smiled.

"Who—who are you?" she said.

"Your servant—Jelerak. I required a disguise in order to reach this place. It amuses me to retain it. I hope that it meets with your approval."

"Indeed," she said, smiling quickly. "When did you arrive?"

"But moments ago," he replied. "I came here directly, to pay my respect and to learn the nature of the difficulty with our Old One."

"The difficulty at the moment," she said, "is that he is quite mad."

"Ah. And how long has this condition prevailed?" he inquired, studying her intently.

"For about half an hour. He anticipated it and told me of it. I was with him when it began."

"I see. Yet the land hereabout has been disturbed by his emanations for a somewhat longer period. How might these be reconciled?"

"Oh." She raised her glass and sipped from it, gestured with her head toward the cabinet. "Please help yourself to a drink, if you'd care to."

"Thank you. I seldom indulge."

She nodded, already knowing this.

"He did it on my instructions."

"That does explain the patterning. I thought I

saw a human mind at work there. Would you care
to tell me why?"

"To keep out the adventurers who have been
trying to break in during your absence. They were
getting to be a nuisance."

"It worked against me also."

"But you had the mirror."

"The mirror was not functioning."

"I began to suspect that only this evening, from
something Baran had said, and I had Tualua clear
it before his lapse. Isn't that how you got here?"

Jelerak shook his head and smiled again.

"I had to do it the hard way. Are you implying
that Baran is up to something that goes against my
interests?"

"I'm not certain. He may have been trying to
repair it for you, also, working to remove some
interference."

"We shall see. Does Tualua's problem mean
what I think it does?"

"His dark nature is rising and he is struggling
against it."

"Hm. Unfortunate, in that it will make him
harder to deal with. Too much egotism will accompany some otherwise laudable sentiments. My
first order of business had better be the restoration
of his sanity so that he can help me to recover from
certain debilities."

"Can you help him at all—beyond temporary re-
lief?"

"Alas, lady, no. For who can triumph over his
own darker nature? You wouldn't know where I
can locate a virgin quickly, would you?"

"No . . . Perhaps one of the younger servants
. . . What do you need one for?"

"Oh, it's going to take a tedious human sacrifice
to straighten out our Old One. It wouldn't if I

were in better form, but that's the way it is just now. Don't worry, I've a virgin locater spell I can use. I'd best be about it right now, as a matter of fact. So I'll take my leave, lady."

"Adieu, Jelerak."

"I may require your services later, as interpreter."

"I will be here."

"Excellent."

He crossed to the door and opened it, smiled back and nodded, went out.

Semirama toyed with her glass, wondering whether the mirror was clear now and how far it could take a person, or persons.

Dilvish regarded the others, and when Lorman's wailing had subsided, he asked, "Do any of you know where I might get my hands on a weapon once I leave here?"

There were a few chuckles, but Hodgson shook his head.

"No. I've no idea where the armory is," he said.

"You would simply have to go looking," Derkon stated. "Good luck. By the way, might I inquire as to your means of egress?"

Dilvish raised a hand to his mouth and withdrew it. He moved it to one of his locks. There came a scraping noise followed by a click.

"A key!" Galt shouted. "He has a key!"

"And the whole castle will know of it if you don't keep your voice down!" Hodgson said. "Where'd you get it, Dilvish?"

"A gift from the lady," he replied, unfastening a second lock and shaking off chains, "making it, in many ways, the most memorable kiss I've ever received."

"Do you," Derkon asked, "think that key might fit other locks than your own?"

"Hard to tell," said Dilvish, bent forward, unfastening his leg fetters.

He straightened and kicked off the chains.

"Here, try it."

Derkon snatched the key and inserted it into one of his locks.

"No, damn it! Perhaps this one . . ."

"Give it here, Derkon! Maybe it fits mine!"

"Over here!"

"Let me try it!"

Derkon tried it on all his locks in succession, while Dilvish was massaging his wrists and ankles, brushing off his garments. Finally, Derkon growled and passed the key to Hodgson.

"There were quite a few keys on the rack outside," Dilvish remarked as Hodgson twisted it within a lock that would not move.

He turned and moved toward the doorway.

"Wait! Wait!"

"Don't go!"

"Get them!"

"Get them!"

He went out. Behind him, their cries turned to curses.

A pale yellow whirlwind sprang up in the center of the room and a variety of exotic aromas filled the place. A number of frogs materialized in the middle of the air and fell to the straw-strewn floor, where they began hopping about. The whirlwind drifted across the chamber, hovered in the doorway.

Moments later a figure appeared behind it, to cast a ring of keys through it to land onto the ledge between Vane and Galt. A brief silence followed, then a chorus of sharp whispers. The figure retreated. The whirlwind turned green. The frogs began to sing.

Dilvish removed a torch from a wall bracket and set out to retrace the course along which he had been dragged. He ignored the cross-tunnels, within which interesting scurryings occurred, even though it seemed that something far back in one called his name in a deep, booming voice. Finally, he came to what seemed the proper turning and headed left, torch flicking, walls dripping, something heavy and leathery bulging from the ceiling and throbbing lightly, as if breathing. He turned again, at the next way which led off to the right. Suddenly, he stopped at another crossway, moving to face each direction in turn. Was this junction here before?

Everything had seemed right up until now, but he had been but semiconscious as they had descended the stair and for a little while afterward . . .

He moistened his left index finger in his mouth and held the torch at arm's distance behind him.

When he raised the finger he felt the cooling movement of the air from left to right. He raised the torch and moved in that direction.

Twenty paces, and he had a choice between a right branch and a left. The left seemed vaguely familiar, so he took it.

Shortly, he found himself at the foot of a stair. Yes. This was the way.

He turned.

As he mounted slowly through the gloom, a lighted doorway came into view above. There was a wall to his left, nothing to his right.

Before he reached the top he extinguished the torch against the wall and dropped it, for the room beyond was clearly illuminated. He heard a faint musical sound coming from around the corner to his right.

He moved slowly, peered around the corner. There was no one in sight, but—

There was *something*, heaped near the torn tapestry, the tiles about it gleaming with a dark wetness.

He sought along the visible sections of wall, hoping for a display weapon of any sort.

Nothing. Mirrors mostly, reflecting the hall and reflections of the hall within one another.

The thing on the floor did not stir. The wet area about it seemed a little larger.

He advanced soundlessly, approaching the dark heap. Partway there, he froze. It was a demon—the one which had come for him in the mucky prison of the pond—its body squashed like a piece of fruit, twisted and broken.

He moved no nearer, but only stood regarding it, wondering. Then he backed away. The odor of its ichor had reached his nostrils. He looked over his shoulder and down the length of the hall. There was a wide entranceway far along it and to the left, a small door to the right, huge double doors at the end. An uncomfortable feeling boiled up within him. He had no desire to pass through that hall.

Before him, past the infernal remains, to the left of the tapestry, was a recess containing a partly open door. Detouring as widely as he could about the broken creature, he headed in that direction.

There was silence and dimness beyond the door. He pushed it open far enough to pass through, and then he let it swing slowly back to its former position. It creaked slightly as it moved in both directions.

He passed along a narrow corridor and veils of violet mist drifted past him, accompanied by sounds like glass wind-chimes and the odors of a mown field. He passed a scullery, a pantry, a small bed-

room, and an octagonal chamber where a blue
flame burned without support above a star-shaped
slab of pink stone. All of these rooms were empty
of people.

At length, the corridor opened upon a larger
one running to the right and the left. Voices reached
him from somewhere to the left and he halted,
listening. The words were indistinguishable and
sufficiently muffled that he chanced a look about
the corner.

There was no one in sight. The sounds seemed
to be coming from one of several opened doors
along that way.

He moved in that direction, staying close to
the wall, looking for some object, some niche, for
concealment, should someone step out of that room.
Nothing, however, presented itself, though by this
time the words were coming clear and he gained
the impression that these were servants' quarters.

It was several minutes before he heard anything
of interest, however.

". . . and I say he's back," said a gruff male voice.

"Just because the messing stopped for a time?"
a woman responded.

"Exactly. It was to let him pass in."

"Then why's no one seen him?"

"Why should he be showin' himself to the likes
of us? Most likely he's up with Baran or the queen,
or both of 'em."

Though he listened for many minutes more, he
heard nothing that proved of additional value. Still,
the one reference was obviously to Jelerak, and
"up" might indicate a higher floor. Dilvish sidled
away, turned, headed in the other direction.

He wandered cautiously for a quarter of an
hour before he came upon a stairway. Then he

waited beneath it for a long while, listening, before he set foot upon it and raced upward.

This upstairs hallway was wide, no mere corridor, was carpeted, was hung with sumptuous tapestries. Dilvish moved along it, seeking a weapon, seeking a voice. He came to a window. He paused.

Yellow fogs rolled by without, revealing and concealing a turbulent landscape lit by moonlight and sporadic bursts of flame, above which glinting blue and white diamond shapes drifted and dipped like wingless, featureless birds riding the air currents. Dark, strong prominences grew in the matter of a few eyeblinks; others fell just as rapidly. Occasional lightnings flared, followed by rolls of thunder. If anything, the place looked even worse than it had during his passage through it. He wondered about Black, Arlata, and the sorcerer Weleand. Of them all, only the wretched conjurer seemed to have survived.

He turned away from the spark-shot view of the shuddering world and continued along the hallway, coming at length to another wide, carpeted stair rising from below, turning, continuing on up. On the wall above the landing hung a pair of large halberds. He crossed to them, took hold of the haft of the nearer one with both hands, raised it, shook his head and carefully fitted the weapon back into place upon its pegs. Too heavy. He'd wear himself out lugging the big thing about.

He passed on, and a warm wind blew by him and the walls seemed to waver. A splashing torrent rounded the corner ahead and a wall of water rushed in his direction. He turned to retreat, but it vanished before it reached him. The walls and floor were dry when he came to the end of the hallway, with only a few flapping fish about.

When he turned the corner, however, there were several puddles. A ghostly arm rose up out of one, holding a blade. Dilvish strode forward and snatched it away. The arm vanished and the blade immediately began to melt. It was made of ice. He dropped it back into the puddle and moved away.

There were a number of doors along the hallway, several of them partly ajar, several closed. He paused and listened outside each of them, hearing nothing, peering into those which stood open. Then he returned to the first of the closed ones and tried it. It was locked, as was the second, the third.

He moved to the end of the hallway where a low stair angled up obliquely to his left. He mounted the stair quickly. The ceiling was lower here, but the carpet and wall hangings were richer. A narrow window gave him a view back upon a portion of the castle itself. It seemed that ghostly figures moved along the battlements above. No doors gave upon this hallway and he hurried through it quickly, mounting another low stair moving off to his left, leading to a high-ceilinged hallway, better illuminated and far more sumptuously furnished than any he had yet seen or traversed.

The first door to his right was locked, but the second was not. He hesitated as it yielded a fraction of an inch to his pressure, overcome by an intuitive certainty that the room beyond was occupied.

He checked his resolution and found that it had not wavered. If Jelerak were within and all else failed, he was still determined to employ his weapon of last resort, the Awful Sayings which would destroy the castle and everything in it—himself included—in the fires that could not be quenched until everything within range of the spell had been reduced to powder and ashes.

He pushed the door open and strode forward.

"Selar! You have come!" Semirama cried, and a moment later she was in his arms.

CHAPTER

VIII

THE large man with curly hair and beard, and with a raw gash running across his left shoulder and down his breast and rib cage on that side, stalked through the tunnels beneath the Castle Timeless, his great blade in his hand. Fighting in the dark, he had already dispatched a nameless leathery monstrosity which had fallen upon him silently from above, in one of the passages farther back. He still moved in darkness, the pupils of his eyes abnormally dilated. His cursing strangely resembled that of Melbriniononsadsazzersteldregandishfeltselior, whom he had met in the hall above with less silence but equal effect. He cursed because he had successfully followed a scent down into these tunnels until he had come to the place where the passage of hordes of piglike creatures had hopelessly muddled the odor-patterns. Now he was lost and could only wander aimlessly until he picked up the trail once again.

The most infuriating thing, however, was that

he was certain that he had seen his man awhile back, rushing past on one of the crossways. He had even called out his name, but gotten no response. By the time he had reached that point, the man was out of sight, and though he had followed his trail successfully for a time after that, the cursed pig-smell had met, mingled with, and submerged it.

He came to a cross-tunnel and turned left and left again at the next one. The choices did not seem to be that important. The only really important thing was to keep moving. Sooner or later . . .

Voices!

He turned. No. They were somewhere ahead, not behind.

He moved on quickly and they grew louder. He spied another crossing of the tunnels ahead and rushed to stand at their center. Turning slowly then, he finally came to face down the one which ran off to his right.

Yes.

There was a bend, a twist. Somewhere beyond it people were moving, talking. He walked that way, not really hurrying. A small illumination had already crept partway toward him.

As he moved about the bend, he saw the men. They were passing from right to left along another cross-tunnel, the man at their head holding a torch high. There might have been half a dozen of them, including an old one. He could not make out their words, but they seemed happy. They were also ragged, and as he drew nearer he realized that their scents were very powerful, as if they had been long pent in a place totally lacking in sanitary facilities.

He stood in darkness and watched them pass. Before very long, he stood in the tunnel down which they had moved. Then he turned in the direction from which they had come and moved off along it.

Shortly, he stood in a large room where a single torch burned low in its bracket. To his left stood a rack of chains and locks. A few torture implements lay dusty in various corners.

The trail led across the room and through an open doorway. Mingled with it, here, was also the scent that he sought. It had been with him for some time, actually, once he had turned upon this way. But here it was stronger, and beyond the doorway . . .

He paused upon the threshold, looking in. The chamber was empty. Its light still burned. Empty chains hung from rings upon the wall. Locks had been cast all over the floor.

He began to move forward and halted again.

That floor . . .

Extending his blade, he brushed aside bunches of rushes and straw. There was something stretched upon the ground beneath it. Something vaguely familiar . . .

His breath caught suddenly and he drew back as if shocked. Perspiration broke out upon his brow and he muttered an imprecation.

He snatched back his blade and sheathed it.

Then he withdrew and retraced his steps up the corridor, easily following the powerful man-smell the others had left. He doubted that even the pig-things could smother it completely.

Jelerak stood before the small brass bowl atop the tripod. Seventeen ingredients, of various degrees of unsavoriness, smoldered within it, and pungent trails of smoke rose before him, coiled past, not entirely unpleasant in aroma. He spoke the words and commenced repeating them at a faster tempo. Small crackling sounds occurred within the bowl and an occasional spark shot forth.

A link had been created, and a subtle psychic pressure began to build within him and the subject of his attentions.

When he came again to the end he recommenced his speaking, this time in an even louder voice and at a yet faster pace. The sputtering and flashing of the compound was now a steady thing. As he neared the end this time, he threw his arms wide, became stiffly immobile, and snapped out the final words in a voice close to a shout.

The smoke swirled for an instant, and the substance within the bowl, which had assumed a steady cherry-colored glow, flashed brightly and emitted a pulse of light which rose to hover in the air above it, taking on the form of a scarlet letter, the runic beginning of the word "virgin."

When it had stabilized, Jelerak spoke a brief command and the bright sign drifted slowly away from him. His arms fell and the tension went out of his body. He placed a cover upon the bowl and moved to follow his creation, through an archway, down a corridor.

It flowed along at eye level, a bright ray upon some errant breeze, a sun-pinked sail upon a dark sea, and Jelerak strolled behind it, smiling with the left side of his mouth.

It wound among the labyrinthine corridors in a vaguely southerly direction, dropping into the first stairwell they came upon. Hands in his pockets now, Jelerak trotted down the steps behind it, all the way to the ground floor. Without hesitation, it turned left and so did he.

He followed it past the enclaves of brightness, where the tapers burned, his shadow growing and shrinking, doubling and twisting—ranging from that of a giant to that of a horned dwarf. He yawned delicately as he passed the tub of the writhing shrub—a rival sorcerer he had long ago transformed and afflicted with aphids. He broke off a leaf as he passed. A drop of blood formed on the stem.

A bat flapped by, dipping near him in greeting. Spiders danced upon ledges and rats raced to keep him company.

Finally, the letter passed through an archway and into the main hall, where its glow was caught in reflection until Jelerak entered there and all of the mirrors went black.

It led him across the front of the hall, coming at last to hover before the great main gate. Jelerak's brow furrowed and he halted for a moment behind it. Then he spoke a guide-word and the letter slid to the right and floated through the door of the side room. The ticking of the big clock was loud about him for a moment as he followed it.

It crossed the shadow-decked room and halted before the lesser door in the front wall.

Still frowning, Jelerak opened the door and looked beyond it as the letter drifted out. The area near the castle remained stable, though beyond a certain point below, the land heaved and twisted, sharp explosions occurred and baleful fires drifted among sulfurous fogs. The moon was already high and wearing a topaz mask. The stars in their grand scatter seemed diminished, more distant . . .

Jelerak followed it outside, the ground trembling slightly beneath his feet. It moved now toward a rough semblance of a trail leading downward among rocks toward the place occupied earlier by a pond, where now a small mountain was reared. A cold wind whipped his cloak about him as he hastened with nimble-footed stride down the alley of boulders.

Partly down the face of the slope, the letter drifted upward to the right, moving across an irregular, sharply angled slope. Jelerak hesitated only a moment and began climbing after it.

Staying close to the slope, it continued its southward drift. Then, abruptly, it vanished.

Jelerak increased his pace, moving rapidly until he caught sight of it again. It had moved around a boulder and now hung in the air before a cleft in the rocks. A faint light emerged from the opening.

As he drew nearer he could see more and more by its glow; until finally, when he stood before it, a blaze of baleful light reached his eyes. The bright rune moved from side to side as if reluctant to enter there. Jelerak spoke another word, however, and it proceeded into the opening.

He followed it, and the rune vanished again, around a bend to the left. When he had made the turn himself, he halted and stared.

A wall of flames completely screened the way before him—dark red, almost oily, braiding and unbraiding itself, silent, feeding upon nothing visible, a faint odor of brimstone about it. The rune hung unmoving once again, several paces before it.

Jelerak stepped forward very slowly, hands upraised, palms outward. He halted when they were about a foot away from the curtains of fire and began moving them in small circles, up and down and to either side.

" 'Tis not the Old One's, my pet," he addressed the letter. "Not an emanation, but a bona fide spell, of a most peculiar sort. However . . . Everything has its weakness, doesn't it?" he finished, curving his fingers suddenly and plunging his hands ahead.

Immediately, he drew his hands to either side, and the flames parted like a slit arras. He gestured with each hand in turn, rotating the wrists, clicking the fingers.

The fires remained in the parted position. The letter flashed past him.

Stepping forward, Jelerak regarded the sleeping white horse and the sleeping blonde-haired girl he had rescued from glassy statuedom for Dilvish. The letter had affixed itself to her brow and was now beginning to fade.

He knelt, lowering his face to scrutinize her more closely. Then he drew back his hand and slapped her.

Her eyes flew open.

"What . . . ? Who . . . ?"

Then she met Jelerak's gaze and grew still.

"Answer my questions," he said. "I last saw you amid shining towers with a man named Dilvish. How did you get here?"

"Where am I?" she responded.

"In a cave, on the slope near the castle. The way was screened by a very interesting protective spell. Who raised it?"

"I do not know," she said, "and I've no idea how I got here."

He peered more deeply into her eyes.

"What is the last thing you remember before the awakening?"

"We were sinking—in the mud—near the pond's edge."

" 'We'? Who else was there?"

"My horse—Stormbird," she said, reaching out and stroking the sleeping animal's neck.

"What became of Dilvish?"

"He crossed the pond with us, was stuck with

us," she said. "But a demon came and dragged him free and bore him off up the hill."

"And that was the last you saw of him?"

"Yes."

"Could you tell whether he was taken into the castle?"

She shook her head.

"I didn't see that."

"Then what happened?"

"I don't know. I woke up here. Just now."

"This grows tedious," Jelerak said, rising. "Get on your feet and come with me."

"Who are you?"

He laughed.

"One who requires a special service of you. This way!"

He gestured back along the route he had come. Her mouth tightened and she rose.

"No," she said. "I am not going with you unless I know who you are and what you want of me."

"You bore me," he said, and he raised his hand.

Almost simultaneously, she raised hers in a gesture closely resembling his own.

"Ah! You *do* know something of the Art."

"I believe you will find me as well equipped as many."

"Sleep!" he announced suddenly, and her eyes closed. She swayed. "Open your eyes now and do exactly as I say: follow me.

"So much for democracy," he added as he turned away, and she fell into step behind him.

He led her out into the night and along the steep way to the trail, by the light of the changing land.

They followed Lorman, and Lorman followed the emanations. Up the shadowy stairway and across the rear of the hall, pausing only to survey the ruined form of their late demonic tormenter with a mixture of dismay and delight, they made their way along a narrow passage, turning right at its farther end.

They passed a stairway and continued on, working their way to the front of the building and heading in a northerly direction.

"I am beginning to feel it," Derkon whispered to Hodgson.

"What?" the other asked.

"The sense of an enormous, mad presence. A feeling of the great power that the thing is pouring forth, rocking the land outside. I—it's frightening."

"That, at least, is a feeling I share with you."

Odil said nothing. Galt and Vane, holding hands, brought up the rear. The walls shimmered, growing transparent in places, and ghostly shapes danced within their depths. Clouds of green smoke puffed past them, leaving them gagging. A huge furry face regarded them solemnly through a hole in the ceiling, vanishing moments later with a flash of fire and a peal of laughter.

At the first window they passed, they viewed the changing land without, where skeletal horsemen raced their skeletal horses through the swirling smoke in the sky.

"We draw nearer!" Lorman croaked, in a voice the others considered overloud.

They came at last to a gallery whose long row of windows afforded numerous views of the altering prospect. The gallery itself was an empty, quiet place, free of the unnatural disturbances they had witnessed during their long walk. Immediately they entered it, all of them were stricken by a sense of the presence Derkon had felt earlier.

"This is the place, isn't it?" he asked.

"No," Lorman replied. "The place is up ahead. There mad Tualua dreams, sending his nightmares to ravage the world. There are two other connecting galleries, it seems. The northernmost may actually be best for purposes of our operation. It will mean passing through his chamber to reach it. But once we have done that, the way should be clear before us."

"If we succeed and live," Odil inquired, "*are* we going to try to kill him during the disturbance that follows?"

"I would hate to waste all of that power . . ." said Vane.

". . . when we've been through so much for it already," said Galt.

"We've the oath to keep us honest," said Lorman, giggling.

"Of course," said Derkon.

Hodgson nodded.

"So long as I have a say in it," said he, "some of it will be used properly."

"All right," said Odil, his voice wavering.

They moved through the gallery, slowing as they passed the windows to view the fire-shot disorder. Coming at last to the Chamber of the Pit, they stayed near the wall as they moved through. An occasional splashing sound occurred within its depths.

They glanced at one another, backs to the wall, as they sidled along. No one spoke. It was not until they had passed beyond the Chamber and reached the entrance to the far gallery that some of them realized that they had all been holding their breath.

They retreated quickly along the farther gallery, turning the first corner they came to, to put the Chamber out of sight. They found themselves in a large, dim alcove across from another bank of windows which let upon a lower, more lava-filled aspect of the changing land.

"Good," Lorman announced, pacing about the area. "The emanations are strong here. We must form ourselves into a circle. It will be a fairly simple matter of focusing, and I will take care of its direction. No. You—Hodgson—over here. You will speak the final words of Undoing. It will be best to have a white magician for that. Derkon, over there! We will each have our parts in this thing. I will assign them in a moment. We will become a lens. Over there, Odil."

One by one, the six magicians took their places in the glare of the burning land. A headless wraith, followed by portions of five other portents, drifted past the windows, the final one beating upon a drum in time with the eruptions below.

"Is that a good omen or a bad one?" Galt asked Vane.

"As with most omens," the other replied, "it is difficult to be certain until it is too late."

"I was afraid you'd say that."

"Attend me now," Lorman stated. "Here are your parts . . ."

Dilvish was propped on one elbow. Semirama smiled up at him.

"Son of Selar," she said, "it was worth whatever may come, to meet you and know you, who are so like that other." She adjusted the bedclothes and continued. "I do not like believing what I now believe about Jelerak, who has always been a friend. But I had come to suspect as much before your arrival. Yes, cruelties were common in my day, too, and I had long grown used to them. And I had no other loyalties in this time and place . . .

"Now—" She sat up. "Now I feel that the time has come to depart and leave him to his own devices. Before long, even the Old One will turn upon him. He will be too occupied then to pursue us. The transport mirror has been cleared. Come flee with me through it. With your sword and certain forces I command, we will soon win us a kingdom."

Dilvish shook his head slowly.

"I've a quarrel with Jelerak which must be settled before I depart this place," he said. "And speaking of blades, I could use one."

She leaned forward and put her arms about him.

"Why must you be so like your ancestor?" she said. "I warned Selar not to go to Shoredan. I knew what would happen. Now to find you, then to have you rush off to your doom in the same fashion . . . Is your entire line cursed, or is it only me?"

He held her and said, "I must."

"That is what he said also, under very similar circumstances. I feel as if I am suddenly rereading an old book."

"Then I hope the current edition has a slightly improved ending. Do not make my part any harder than it is already."

"That I can always handle," she said, smiling, "if we are together. If you attempt this thing and succeed, will you take me away with you?"

He regarded her in the strange light which was now entering through the windows at his back, and as had his ancestor an age before him, he answered, "Yes."

Later, when they had risen and repaired their costumes and Semirama had sent Lisha to locate a weapon, they drank a glass of wine and her thoughts turned again to Jelerak.

"He has fallen," she said, "from a high place. I do not ask you to forgive where you cannot, but remember that he was not always as he is now. For a time, he and Selar were even friends."

"For a time?"

"They quarreled later. Over what, I never knew. But yet, it was so, in those days."

Dilvish, leaning against a bedpost, stared into his glass.

"This gives rise to a strange thought," he said.

"What is it?"

"The time we met, he might simply have brushed me aside—slain me on the spot, cast me into a sleep, turned my mind away from him as if he were not there. I wonder . . . Might it have been my resemblance to Selar that caused him to be particularly cruel?"

She shook her head.

"Who can say? I wonder whether even he knows the full reasons for everything he does."

She took a sip of wine, rolled it about her mouth.

"Do you?" she added, swallowing.

Dilvish smiled.

"Does anyone? I know enough to satisfy my judgment in the matter. Perfect knowledge I leave to the gods."

"Generous of you," she said.

There came a soft knock upon the door.

"Yes?" she called out.

"It is I. Lisha."

"Come in."

The woman entered, bearing something wrapped in a green shawl.

"You found one?"

"Several. From an upstairs chamber one of the others had shown me."

She unwound the shawl, revealing three blades.

Dilvish finished his drink and put the glass down. He moved forward and took up each of the weapons in turn.

"This one's for show."

He set it aside.

"This one has a good guard, but the other is a bit heavier and has a better point. Though this one's sharper . . ."

He swung both of them, tried them both in his sheath, decided upon the second. Then he turned and embraced Semirama.

"Wait," he said. "Have some things ready for a quick journey. Who knows how this will all fall out?"

He kissed her and strode to the door.

"Goodbye," she said.

As he moved along the hallway, a peculiar feeling possessed him. None of the creaks or scratchings which had been present earlier were now to be heard. An unnatural stillness lay upon the place—a tense, vibrant thing, like the silence between the peals of a great-throated bell. Imminence and impendency rode like electric beings past him; in their wake came panic, which he fought without understanding, his new blade half drawn, knuckles white as he gripped it.

Baran uttered an oath for the seventh time and seated himself upon the floor in the midst of his paraphernalia. Tears of frustration rose in his eyes and ran down on either side of his nose, losing themselves in his mustache.

Couldn't he do anything right today? Seven times he had summoned elementals, charged them and sent them into Jelerak's mirror. Almost immediately, each had vanished. Something was keeping the mirror open now. Could it be Jelerak himself, getting ready to return? Might not Jelerak appear within it and step out of the frame at any moment, his ancient eyes staring unblinking into his own, reading every secret of his soul as if they were all branded upon his brow?

Baran sobbed. It was so unfair, to be caught in one's treachery before it was brought to a successful conclusion. Any moment now . . .

Yet Jelerak did not appear behind the glass. The world had not yet ended. It might even be that some other force was responsible for the destruction of his elementals.

What, then?

He shook his mind free of the feelings, forcing himself to think. If it was not Jelerak, it had to be someone else. Who?

Another sorcerer, of course. A powerful one. One who had decided that the time had come to enter here and take charge . . .

Yet no other face than his own regarded him from the glass. What was that other one waiting for?

Puzzling. Irritating. If it were a stranger, could he make a deal? he wondered. He knew a lot about this place. He was an accomplished sorcerer himself . . . Why didn't something happen?

He rubbed his eyes. He hauled himself to his feet. This had been a very dissatisfying day.

Crossing to a small window, he looked out. It was several moments before he realized that something was not right, and several more before it struck him as to what it was.

The changing land had again stopped changing. The land lay smoking but still beneath the racing moon. When had this occurred? It could not have been very long ago . . .

This stoppage signified another lull in Tualua's

consciousness. Now might well be the time to move in, to take control. He had to get downstairs, get hold of that bitch queen, drag her to the Pit —before someone came through the mirror and beat him to it. As he hurried across the room, he reviewed the binding spell he had outlined.

As he reached toward the door, a strange tension came into him, and with it a return of his vertigo in a key at which he had never experienced it before.

No! Not now! No!

But even as he flung the door wide and rushed toward the stair, he knew that this time it was different. There was something more to it than a recurrence of all his old fears, something—premonitory, which even his earlier spells were now seen as leading up to. It was as if the entire castle were, in some sense, holding its breath against a monumental occurrence the moment for which was almost at hand. It was as if this—foreboding—had in some measure communicated itself even to mighty Tualua, shocking him into momentary quiescence. It was—

He came to the top of the stair, looked down, and shuddered. His entire nature seemed, at the moment, riven.

He ground his teeth, put out his hand, and took the first step . . .

Monstrously ancient structures of an imposing nature are not in the habit of having been constructed by men. Nor was the Castle Timeless an exception, as most venerable cities trace their origins to the architectural enterprise of gods and demigods, so the heavy structure in the Kannais which predated them all, and which had over the ages served every conceivable function from royal palace to prison, brothel to university, monastery to abandoned haunt of ghouls—changing even its shape, it was said, to accommodate its users' needs —so it informed with the echoes of all the ages, was muttered by some (with averted eyes and evil-forfending gesture) to be a relic of the days when the Elder Gods walked the earth, a point of their contact with it, a toy, a machine, or perhaps even a strangely living entity, fashioned by those higher powers whose vision transcended that of mankind—whom they had blessed or cursed with the spark of self-consciousness and the ache of curiosity that was the beginning of soul—as mankind's surpassed that of the hairy tree-dwellers counted by some as his kin, for purposes best known only to those shining folk whom it at least served somewhere, somehow as an interdimensional clubhouse before those beings absented themselves to felicity of a higher order, leaving behind the unripened fruits of their meddling in the affairs of otherwise satisfied simians; fashioned, in the opinion of some metaphysicians, on a timeless plane out of spiritual substances and, hence, not truly a part of this grosser world to which it had been transported, consisting as it did of equal measures of good and evil and their more interesting counterparts, love and hate, compounded with a beauty, therefore, that was both sinister and beatific, possessed of an aura as absorbent as a psychic sponge and as discriminating, alive in the sense that a man with only a functioning portion of his right hemisphere might be said to live, and anchored in space and time by an act of will imperfect because divided, yet superior to normal earthly vicissitudes for all the unearthly reasons the metaphysician would not care to recite a second time.

This, of course, was all wrong, according to

more practical-minded theorists. Old buildings might acquire a patina of use, even exceptionally well-constructed ones, and their ambience had much to do with any physical or psychic impressions to be gained within their walls—particularly those situated in mountainous areas prone to a wide range of meteorological influences. And yes, when such people inhabited the place, it performed almost completely in accord with their expectations, as did the world at large. Such was its sensitivity.

Filled with sorcerers and demons, home to an Old One, it changed again. Other aspects of its nature were called forth.

A test of its true nature, of course, arose when the imperfect will upon which it resided was challenged, just as the proof of the evil or the good lay in the doing.

CHAPTER

IX

HUMMING softly to himself, Jelerak leaned far forward, pushing the wheelbarrow in a low plane so as not to jar its occupant loose. Still entranced, Arlata of Marinta lay spread-eagled in the conveyance, her legs strapped to the handles, her arms hanging over the sides, drawn downward and secured to the traces near the wheel. A large quantity of sacking had first been stuffed into the barrow beneath her shoulders so as to provide for a proper spreading of the rib cage. Her tunic had been opened and a red dotted line painted to bisect her upper abdomen in the substernal area. A rattling sack of instruments lay across her stomach.

He moved along the east-west corridor leading to the Chamber of the Pit, and hordes of vermin trailed behind him with a gleeful chittering. The air grew warmer and more humid as he advanced, and the odor of the place was already heavy. Smiling, he pushed the wheelbarrow through the last few feet of shadow and passed beyond the low archway into the chamber itself.

He continued on across the dung-streaked floor, to position the barrow carefully near the eastern edge of the pit. Straightening then, he stretched, sighed, and yawned in that order, before opening the sack and removing three long spokes and a fastener, which he quickly assembled into a tripod. Setting it on the floor between the barrow's handles, he placed his favorite brass bowl atop it and dumped smoldering charcoal into it from a small, perforated bucket which had hung from the barrow's right handle. He blew upon it until it produced a cheery glow, and then from several small sacks he introduced quantities of powder and herbs which caused a thick, sickly smoke to pour forth, sweet-smelling and slow-coiling, about the area.

Rats came from lurking places to pirouette upon the flagstones as he resumed his humming and withdrew a short, wide, triangular-bladed knife from the sack, tested its point and edges with his thumb, placed its tip for a moment at the top of the line he had drawn beginning between Arlata's pink-tipped breasts, smiled, nodded, and set it down upon her stomach for future use. Next, he removed a brush and several small, sealed pots, shook down the sack, placed it upon the floor beside him, opened one of the pots and knelt.

Bats dipped and darted as his hand dipped and darted, beginning with sure, practiced movements the painting of an elaborate design in red.

As he worked, a sudden chill passed over him, and the rats halted their dancing. The squeaking, chirping noises ceased and a moment of profound silence slipped into being, bearing a terrible tension within it. It was almost as if a sound, high above the range of audibility, were slowly descending in pitch toward the point where it would shortly become an unbearable shriek.

He cocked his head as if listening. He looked at the pit. More of the Old One's unnatural rantings, of course. This would soon be set aright, when he tore the heart out of the girl and poured her life force like oil upon the troubled waters of the Old One's mind—at least for a time. At least long enough to obtain the succor he himself would then require of that one's stable and directed energies. Afterward . . .

He wondered how a creature like that would die. Effecting this state of affairs might take a lot of doing. But soon Tualua would be growing dangerous, not only to the rest of the world but specifically to him, Jelerak, personally. He licked his lips as he foresaw the epic battle which must occur one day soon. He knew that he would not emerge from it unscathed, but he also knew that if he could drain the Old One's life energies, his power would reach a peak he had never before attained—godlike, he would rival Hohorga himself . . .

His face darkened at the thought of his former enemy and later master. And, fleetingly, he recalled Selar, who had given his life to slay that mighty being. Odd, how that one's features had echoed down the ages, to find a home on the face of the man he had sent to Hell, the man who had somehow returned from that foul place, the man who had saved him from the changing land as Selar had long ago drawn him back from the Nungen Abyss—Selar, who had found favor in the eyes of Semirama . . . And Dilvish might still be about— somewhere near, even—which was why he needed his full powers again quickly. That one was of godslayer's blood, and for the first time was causing Jelerak to know twinges of fear.

He continued the construction of a ritual diagram, no longer humming, tearing open another pigment pot when the first was exhausted.

Then, borne upon a stray air current through the unnatural silence, a faint sound came to him. It was as if a masculine chorus were somewhere raised in a naggingly familiar chant. He paused in mid-stroke, straining to catch the pattern, if not the words, to the piece.

A focusing spell. A very standard article . . .

But who were they? And what was it they were attempting to focus?

He looked down at his almost completed diagram. It was not good to have too many magical operations going on within the same area. They sometimes had a way of interfering with one another. Yet at this point he was loath to have his own work undone, so close to completion. He did a rapid mental-spiritual juggling act, a calculation of possible potentials, a balancing of forces.

It should not matter. The outpourings of energy here would be on such a scale that he could see very little that could unbalance the work, even at close proximity. He began painting again with tight-lipped fury. As soon as this business was out of the way, that damned choir was going to learn something about fates worse than death. He rehearsed a few of these to calm and amuse himself as he painted in the final sections. Then he rose, surveyed his work, and saw that it was good.

He backed off, setting his painting equipment aside, then entered the pattern in the proper fashion, moving to the south side of the wheelbarrow —Arlata's right—the brazier smoking and steaming to his right, cleared his head, spoke several words

of power, then reached down and picked up the
sacrificial blade.

The bats and rats resumed their darting capers
as he began the preamble to the directions which
would form the spell, and the consecration of the
blade which would give it life. Crashing sounds
began about the chamber and a scratching noise
crossed the ceiling. He raised the blade as he spoke
the words, drowning out the voices in the distance
—or had they already ceased of their own accord?
The trail of smoke became depressed, crossing his
pattern like an inquisitive serpent. A general creaking began within the walls.

The superauditory rushing he had sensed earlier
seemed about to burst into voice. He shifted his
grip upon the blade and enunciated the next eleven
words in a voice of beautiful plangency.

Then he froze, shaking, as his name was spoken
by a curly-bearded man who had to duck his head
to pass beneath the archway:

"There you are, Jelerak, as I should have guessed
I'd find you—surrounded by toads, bats, snakes,
spiders, rats and noxious fumes, next to a big pool
of shit, about to tear out a girl's heart!"

Jelerak lowered the blade.

"These are a few of my favorite things," he
said, smiling, "and you—lout!—are not among
them!"

The blade began to crackle with a hellish light
as he turned to point it at the giant in the doorway.

Then the flames on the blade died, and all else
that was light in the chamber was darkened as the
scream reached audibility—a piercing thing that
went on and on, casting both men to the floor,
causing even great Tualua to commence thrashing
within his pit, reaching the point where all who

heard it were deafened before they lapsed into unconsciousness.

Finally, a pale light came into the still chamber. It brightened and brightened, then faded and went away.

Then it came again . . .

Hodgson awoke with a mighty headache. For a time he just lay there, trying to think of a spell to make it go away. But his thinking machinery was sluggish. Then he heard the moaning and a soft sobbing. He opened his eyes.

A pale light filled the alcove. It brightened perceptibly even as he looked about him. Old Lorman lay nearby, head turned to the side, a pool of blood below his open mouth. He was not breathing. Derkon was sprawled some distance beyond him. It was his moaning that Hodgson had heard. Odil was breathing, but still obviously unconscious.

He turned his head to the left, toward the source of the sobbing.

Vane was sitting, his back against the wall, Galt's head in his lap. Galt's features were frozen in a look of agony. His limbs had the loose, floppy quality of the recent dead. His chest neither rose nor fell. Vane looked down upon him, making small, rocking movements, his breath coming quickly, his eyes moist.

The light reached the intensity of full daylight.

As there was nothing he could do for Lorman or Galt, he crawled past the former and came up beside Derkon. He inspected the man's head for lacerations, found a red swollen area high and left on his forehead.

A small healing spell then occurred to him. He repeated it three times upon his companion before the moaning stopped. His own headache began to subside while he worked with it. The light had grown noticeably dimmer by then.

Derkon opened his eyes.

"Did it work?" he asked.

"I don't know," Hodgson replied. "I'm not sure what its effects should be."

"I've some idea," said Derkon, sitting up, rubbing his head and neck, standing. "We can check it out in a minute."

He looked around him. He went over and kicked Odil on the side.

Odil rolled over onto his back and looked up at him.

"Wake up when you get a chance," Derkon said.

"What—what's happened?"

"I don't know. Galt and Lorman are dead, though." He looked toward the window, stared, rubbed his eyes and walked off quickly in that direction. "Come here!" he cried.

Hodgson followed him. Odil was still in the process of sitting up.

Hodgson arrived at the window just in time to see the sun plunge out of sight beyond the western mountains. The sky was filled with wheeling points of light.

"Fastest sunset I ever saw," Derkon remarked.

"The whole sky seems to be turning. Look at the stars."

Derkon leaned against the window frame.

"The land has calmed down," he remarked.

A broken white ball rolled down out of the sky behind the mountains.

"Was that what I think it was?"

"Looked like the moon to me," said Hodgson.

"Oh, my!" said Odil, staggering up and leaning

upon the sill just as a pale light suffused the heavens and the stars went away. "I don't feel well."

"Obviously," Derkon said. "It took you all night to get here."

"I don't understand."

"Look," Derkon said, gesturing, as shadows swirled about every feature of the landscape and clouds blossomed and blew themselves apart.

A golden ball of fire raced cometlike across the sky.

"Do you think it's speeding up?" Hodgson asked.

"Possibly. Yes. Yes, I do."

The sun passed behind the mountains and the darkness came on again.

"We've been standing here all day," Hodgson said to Odil.

"Gods! What have we done?" Odil asked, unable to take his eyes off the wheeling heavens.

"We've broken the maintenance spell of the Castle Timeless," Hodgson answered. "Now we know what it was maintaining."

"And why the place was called the Castle Timeless," Derkon added.

"What are we going to do? Attempt the binding?"

"Later. I'm going to try to find something to eat first," said Derkon, moving away. "It's been days . . ."

After a time, the others turned and followed him. Vane still rocked gently, stroking Galt's brow as another night passed.

Dilvish awoke upon a heavy, bright-patterned carpet, his blade still clutched tightly in his right hand. He had difficulty in opening it. He rubbed his hand after he had sheathed the weapon and tried to recall what had happened.

There had been a scream. Oh, yes. A wail of pain and anger. He had halted before the partly opened door of a room—this room?—when it began.

He sat up and was able to view the hallway's west window through the opened door, as well as an east window on the room's far wall, to his right. A curious phenomenon then became apparent. First, the window on the right grew bright while the one on the left was still dim. Then the right window dimmed as the left one brightened. Then the left one grew dark. Shortly, the one to the right brightened again and the sequence was repeated. He sat unmoving, save for the flexing of his hand as it recurred several times more.

Finally, he rose to his feet and moved to the east window in time to see the sky inscribed with a countless number of bright concentric circles. Moments later, they fled before a tower of flame that came up out of the east and mounted toward midheaven.

He shook his head. The land itself seemed to have grown calm. What new device was this? The work of his enemy? Or something else?

Turning away, he passed through the door and out into the hall again. The light-dark succession continued beyond the bank of windows to his left. When he glanced back, he could no longer see the door he had just passed through, but only a blank expanse of wall.

He continued on to what he thought had been another passageway going off right angles to the one he trod. Instead, he found himself at the head of a stair covered with a dark, wine-colored carpeting, a wooden banister at either hand.

He descended slowly. The room was filled with

upholstered furniture, and paintings of a sort he had never seen before, in wide, ornate, gilt frames.

He passed through. Dust rose in a huge puff when he rested his hand on the back of one of the chairs.

Turning right, he walked beneath a wooden archway. The next room was a small one, paneled, similarly furnished, and he heard a whooshing sound as he entered.

A small fireplace had just come alive. A bottle of wine, a wedge of cheese, a small loaf of bread and a basket of fruit stood upon a low, round table near the hearth. The chair beside it looked comfortable. Poisoned, perhaps? A trick of the enemy's?

He moved nearer, broke off a crumb of the cheese, sniffed it, tasted it. Then he seated himself and began eating.

His head and eyes moved frequently as he ate, but he saw no one, nothing untoward. Yet it felt as if there were a presence, a beneficent one, in the room with him, guarding him, wishing him well. So strong did the feeling become that he muttered "Thank you" the next time that his mouth was clear. Immediately, the flames leaped and the fire crackled. A wave of pleasant warmth reached him.

Finally he rose and, looking back, was dismayed to discover that the way through which he had entered the room had vanished. Paneling now covered that wall, another of the peculiar pictures hanging upon it—a sun-flooded wood, after a moment's scrutiny, all of the details blurred by a strange kind of loose brushwork of heavy pigments.

"All right," he said, "whoever you are, I take it you are kindly disposed toward me. You have fed me, and it appears that there is some place you would have me go. I must be suspicious of everything within these walls, yet I do feel inclined to trust you. I will go out the only door I see. Lead on, and I will follow."

He crossed to the door and departed the room. He found himself in a long, dim, high hall. There were many doorways, but a soft light shone in only one of them. Dilvish moved in that direction and the light retreated. He walked a short corridor and found himself in another hall similar to the first. This time the light appeared in a doorway far to his left. He crossed the hall diagonally, heading for it.

When he had passed through, he found a corridor running right to left. The light was now somewhere far down to the left. He headed that way.

After several turnings his way debouched into a wide, low hallway with a regular series of narrow windows along its nearer wall. He hesitated there, looking right and left.

Then a pale light passed before him, heading to the right. It winked out almost as soon as he had turned in that direction. He pursued it. It vanished when he set foot upon its trail.

The windows showed him a scene in which swimming clouds had lost their distinction and the sky had taken on a greenish tone, a narrow band of bright yellow arcing from horizon to horizon like the handle of a blazing basket.

Dilvish moved quickly forward, the light beyond the windows pulsing only faintly as he passed.

It was a long hallway, but eventually it led into another—a gallery with wide windows to the right, affording a fuller view of the peculiar sky above a landscape where what must have been daylong storms passed in a matter of eyeblinks, where the trees pulsed green, gold and bone, the ground white and dark, patches of green flickering on and off. It had again become a changing land, but in a manner radically different from the fashion of its previous alterations. What earlier had been barely distinguishable creaking noises were now a steady hum.

An outhouse odor reached his nostrils and he wondered at the dirty trail which ran down the center of the floor. Ahead lay a large, high-ceilinged chamber, and he slowed his pace involuntarily as he neared it. A feeling of foreboding filled him. It was as if a dark and evil aura lay upon that room, as if something brooding, sinister, and—somehow—frustrated dwelt within it, waiting, waiting its opportunity to exercise a unique malice. He shuddered and touched the hilt of his blade, slowing even more as he approached the archway that led inside.

He found himself moving to the left, until he was pressed against that wall, sidling along, finally to halt in the shadowy corner just before the opening.

He edged forward, gripping the weapon now, and peered into the room. At first he saw nothing within the gloom, but then his eyes adjusted to the inferior light and he made out the large, dark, central area of depression within it. Something stood at its left-hand edge, some small object he could not quite distinguish. It was touched for a moment by the glow he had followed earlier, but this light departed almost immediately and he still could not tell what it was that had been so indicated—though the message seemed clear and imperative to him.

Still he hesitated, until a slender tentacle rose up out of the dark place and began groping about its edge, near to the thing he was observing. Then, suddenly moist with perspiration, he forced himself to enter, green boots silent upon the flagstone.

Baran shook his head, spit out a tooth chip, swallowed. The spittle tasted bloody. He spit several times after that and began coughing. His left eye was stuck partly closed. When he rubbed it a dark, caked substance began to flake away. He examined his hand. Dried blood, it was. Then that dully throbbing, seminumb place . . .

He raised his fingertips to the spot on his forehead. Then the pain began. He turned his head this way and that. He lay upon his side at the foot of the stair. So that's what happened when it finally got you . . .

He shifted his bulk preparatory to rising and immediately lapsed back from the pain in his left arm and leg. Damn! he thought. They'd better not be broken! Don't know any spells for broken bones . . .

Trying again, he propped himself only with his right arm and rolled into a seated position, legs extended straight before him. Better, better . . .

He began carefully flexing the leg and feeling it. The pain did not diminish, but nothing seemed broken. Only then did he try exercising his sorcerer's disciplines upon it. The ache started to subside after a few leg movements, becoming only a minor twinge. Then he turned his attention to his scalp and repeated the process with the same result.

Next, he felt along the length of his arm, and a white flash of pain passed through him when he squeezed the left forearm lightly.

All right.

Carefully, very carefully then, he fitted his left hand in between his wide belt and wide stomach.

He began again the exercise that would diminish the pain. When this was completed, he rose cautiously to his feet, his good hand upon the wall. He breathed heavily for a full minute after this, head lowered.

Finally he straightened, took several steps, halted and looked about him. Something was very wrong. There should have been a wall to the left, not a marble balustrade. He followed it with his eyes. It ran for eight or ten paces, then halted next to the head of a wide staircase. A good distance farther along, it began again.

He looked out beyond the balustrade. It was a huge, long room, stone-walled, shadow-hung, with elaborate cornices, with carved capitals atop fluted pilasters. It was furnished in areas, and a dark, long, narrow rug ran its length down the center.

He crossed over, leaned upon the balustrade. There was no trace of his former vertigo. Perhaps it had been exorcised by the fall. Perhaps it had been a premonition of the fall . . .

Strange, how strange . . . He moved his eyes. There had been no such room here before. He had never seen such a room, in Castle Timeless or anywhere else. What had happened?

His gaze found the far corner to his left and froze. Behind a group of high-backed chairs, in an area heavy with shadows, something very large and very still and very black was standing, staring at him. He could tell because the eyes shone redly in the gloom, and they met his own, unblinking, across the distance.

His throat tightened, strangling back a cry that could have continued into hysteria. Whatever the thing was, it was facing a master sorcerer.

He raised his hand and summoned the calm

necessary to precede the storm he was about to unleash.

A faint light began to play about his fingertips as he rehearsed the spell, speaking only the key words of it. When he brought his fingers together, his hand resembled a conical taper in the light that it shed. When he drew his fingertips apart, a downward-curved plane of illumination remained among them and continued, flaring upward, advancing the line of its arc. It ran back upon itself, forming a blazing white sphere to which he issued a guide-word, then cast directly toward the lurker in the shadows.

Trailing sparks and burning in its flight, it moved slowly, almost drifting toward its target.

The shadowy figure did not stir even as it drew near. The light shattered and went out just before it reached it. Then a sweet voice which seemed to come from a point much nearer said, "Very unfriendly, very unfriendly," and the thing wheeled and passed through the adjacent doorway with a quick, clattering sound.

Baran lowered his hand slowly, then raised it to his mouth as he began to cough again. Damned wight! Who had summoned it, anyway? Could it possibly be that Jelerak had returned?

He moved away from the balustrade and headed for the stair.

When he reached the bottom he investigated the corner. In the dust he found the imprint of a cloven hoof.

Holrun cursed and turned onto his stomach, drawing the pillow over his head and pressing down hard upon it.

"No!" he cried. "No! I'm not here! Go away!"

He lay still for a rapid succession of pulsebeats. Then, gradually, the tension went out of him. His hand fell from the pillow. His breathing grew regular.

Abruptly, his form stiffened again.

"No!" he shrieked. "I'm just a poor little sorcerer trying to get some sleep! Leave me alone, damn it!"

This was followed by a growling noise and a clicking of teeth. Finally, his left hand shot forward and drew upon an ivory inlaid drawer set into the head of the bed. It entered, groped a moment, and withdrew carrying a small crystal.

He rolled onto his back, propped the pillow, and squirmed into a semi-upright position. He balanced the shining ball on his abdomen and looked down at it through half-open, sleep-swollen eyes. It took a long while for the image to form within it.

"Make it good," he mumbled. "Make it worth the risk of transformation into a lower life form with a loathsome disease, itching piles, and Saint Vitus' dance. Make it worth the demon-tormentors, the plague of locusts, and the salt in the wounds. Make it—"

"Holrun," said Meliash, "it's important."

"It better be. I'm tireder than the king's whore come the revolution. What do you want?"

"It's gone."

"Good. Who needed it, anyway?"

He moved his hand, preparatory to breaking the connection, paused.

"What's gone?" he inquired.

"The castle."

"The castle? The whole damned castle?"

"Yes."

He was silent a moment. Then he raised himself

further upright, rubbed his eyes, brushed back his hair.

"Tell me about it," he said then, "preferably in simple terms."

"The changing land stopped changing for a time. Then it started in again, wilder than I'd ever seen it before. I got to a good vantage point to watch. After a while, it stopped again. The castle was gone. Everything is still now, and the hilltop is empty. I don't know what happened. I don't know how it happened. That's all."

"Do you think Jel—he was able to move it? If so, why? Or maybe the Old One?"

Meliash shook his head.

"I've been talking with Rawk again. He's turned up more material. There is an old tradition that the place is timeless, was just sort of anchored to time and carried along with it. If that anchor were somehow lifted, it would drift away on the river of eternity."

"Poetic as all hell, but what does it mean?"

"I don't know."

"Do you think that's what happened?"

"I don't know. Maybe."

"Shit!"

Holrun massaged his temples, sighed, picked up the crystal, swung his legs over the bed's edge.

"All right," he said. "All right. I have to look into it. I've come this far. I've got to wash up, though, and eat something first. You've spoken with the other wardens?"

"Yes. They've nothing to add to what I saw."

"Okay. Keep the place under surveillance. Call me immediately if anything new develops."

"Certainly. Are you going to notify the Council?"

Holrun made a face and broke the connection,

wondering whether the Council could be unanchored and set adrift in eternity.

Vane had ceased his sobbing, and for a long while he sat deep in thought, no longer looking at Galt, staring instead at the brightness-dimness sequence in the sky beyond the window. Finally, he stirred.

He lowered Galt's head gently to the floor, then got to his feet. Stooping, he raised his companion's still form into a position across his shoulders.

He moved forward, coming out of the alcove, looked to the right, winced, turned left. Slowly, he advanced along the gallery until he came to a low stair leading upward to his left. Spying a short corridor with several open doors above it, he mounted there.

Moving more slowly, more cautiously, he inspected the rooms. None was occupied. The second and third were bedchambers, the first a sitting room.

He entered the third and, stooping, drew back the coverlet with one hand. He deposited Galt upon the bed and arranged his limbs. He leaned forward and kissed him, then covered him over.

Turning away, he departed the room without looking back, drawing the door closed behind him.

Moving to the right, he came to the end of the corridor, where a low archway opened to the right upon a narrow stair leading downward.

He descended, to find himself in a formal dining room, with four places set at one end of a long table. A basket of bread stood at the head. He seized it and began eating. On a tray beneath a napkin was some sliced meat. He commenced wolfing this down also. An earthen crock nearby contained some red wine, which he drank straight from the pot. Maneuvering about the table as he fed himself, he turned gradually to face back in the direction from which he had come.

The stairway had vanished. The wall was now solid at the point where he had made his entrance. Still chewing vigorously, he crossed over and tapped upon it. It did not sound hollow. He shuddered as he drew back from it. This place . . .

He turned and fled out the double doors at the room's farther end. The hallway was wide, as was the descending stair to which it led. It was decorated with silks and steel, and partly carpeted in green. He reached for the most useful-seeming blade that hung upon the wall—a short, somewhat heavy, double-edged weapon with a simple hilt. As he took it into his hands and turned away to get the feeling of it in motion, he saw that the doors through which he had just departed the dining room had disappeared, to be replaced by a window through which a gentle, pearly light now entered.

He retraced his steps and peered through the panes. A range of mountains was sinking in a place where there had been no mountains before. The sky was now a uniform dead white in color, with neither sun nor stars, as if varying values of illumination had been averaged out above him. A silvery substance rushed forward, halted, moved again. It took some time for him to realize that it was water, creeping nearer. He pulled himself away from the window and headed for the stair.

He fought back the panic which had taken hold of him, replacing it with the hatred he felt for the castle and everything in it. When he reached the foot of the stair, he moved through an anteroom elaborately decorated in a style he did not recognize, though he prided himself upon knowledge of such matters. He halted then upon the threshold to the main hall.

This room also was unoccupied. He was familiar with it from having been brought in this way when captured by the castle's slaves on the slopes below. He and Galt had been dragged before the steward, Baran, routinely abused, and incarcerated below. His hand tightened upon the haft of the weapon as he recalled that day. He moved then, striding across the hall past the great doors, heading toward the sitting room with its smaller entrance to the outside world.

As he neared it he slowed, puzzled. The tall wooden thing with the circular face surrounded by numerals was making a shrill, whining sound. Approaching to study it, he saw that a round, vibrating area existed immediately above the face. He could not determine its character or cause, though it did not seem threatening. He decided against tampering with unknown magics and passed it by, entering the sitting room.

Crossing quickly to the door, he placed his hand upon it, then hesitated. Peculiar things were happening outside. But then, the same might be said for inside also.

He operated the latch and opened the door.

A shrieking, as of some mighty wind, came to his ears. There was water for as far as he could see in every direction of which he commanded a view. Yet the waves and ripples normally present in a large body of water were not distinct here. Perhaps it was the mist of fine spray which seemed to hover above it all . . .

He extended his blade forward, out into the moist haze. An instant later, he jerked it back.

Its tip had entirely rusted away. When he

touched the oxidized fringe that still clung to the metal, it turned to powder beneath his finger and fell free. The screeching continued, deafening. The sky was still an unbroken, nacreous expanse.

He closed the door and latched it, stood with his back against it. He began to tremble.

Having packed the jewels and garments in which she had been buried into a small parcel that now resided beneath the bed, Semirama paced her room deciding whether anything else would be worth taking. Cosmetics?

There came a knock upon the door. She was near. She opened it herself.

Jelerak smiled at her.

"Oh!"

She reddened.

"I am going to have need of your linguistic abilities," he stated.

A pair of rose-tinted goggles hung about his neck. The butt of a scarlet wand protruded from a long, narrow sheath at his belt. He bowed, gesturing toward her left, down the hallway.

"Please come with me."

"Yes—Of course."

She stepped out, began walking alongside him in that direction. She glanced out the window at a pearly sky above an interminable sea.

"Something is the matter?" she asked finally.

"Yes. There was—interference," he replied.

Abruptly, a rushing sound passed overhead, like a clacking of hoofs.

"A huge, dark-haired man interrupted me in the midst of my work," he explained.

"Was that what caused the—spasm? And all these effects?"

He shook his head.

"No, someone has released the maintenance spell and we are no longer a part of the normal flow of time."

"Do you think Tualua did it? Or the stranger?"

He paused to look out another window. The sea had almost completely receded, and now mountain ranges reared themselves even as he watched.

"I do not believe that Tualua was in any condition to do that. And I think the stranger was as surprised by it as I was. But I had a glimpse of the stranger's spirit before I lost consciousness. He was something elemental, demonic, which had only taken human form for a time. This was why I fled as soon as I recovered—to obtain certain tools I had cached." He ran his thumb across the top of the wand. "This is my weapon for dealing with beings such as that. You've seen such before, I'm sure, long ago—"

She gasped. The entire sky flamed a brilliant crimson, became a blinding white. She shielded her eyes and looked away, but it was already dimming.

"What—what was that?"

Jelerak lowered his own hand from his eyes.

"Probably the end of the world," he said.

They watched as the sky continued to dim, until it became a smoky, yellowish color. This persisted. Finally, Jelerak turned away.

"At any rate," he went on, "that one has probably removed my original means of accomplishing Tualua's pacification. So"—he touched the goggles—"these. There was a time when I could have charmed him with my eyes and voice alone, but now I have need to augment my gaze. You must call him, get him to raise himself, so that for a moment we look at one another."

"What then?"

"I must restore the maintenance spell."

"What of whoever broke it?"

"I must regain full force next, find that person, and deal with him."

He began walking again. She fell into step beside him.

"We're really trapped, then," she said. "Even if you do these things, where will it leave us?"

He laughed harshly.

"Even knowledge may have its limits," he said. "On the other hand, I believe that ingenuity is boundless. We shall see."

They walked on, took a stair, took a turn.

"Jelerak," she said, "where did this place come from?"

"We may find that out, too," he replied. "I do not know for certain, though I am beginning to believe that it is—somehow—alive."

She nodded.

"I've had a few peculiar feelings myself. If this is the case, whose side might it be on?"

"Its own, I think."

"It's powerful, isn't it?"

"Look out any window. Yes, there are too many powerful things at work here. I don't like it. I once had my will subjugated to a greater force—"

"I know."

"—and I will not permit it to occur again. It would be the end of both of us—and of many other things."

"I do not understand."

"If my will is broken, your flesh will return to the dust from which I raised it—and other things which depend upon me will fail."

She took his arm.

"You must be careful."

He laughed again.

"The battle is barely begun."

Her grip tightened upon his arm.

"But the trip may be ending. Look!"

She pointed ahead to a window through which a very pale sun-arch had appeared in a twilit sky.

She felt him stiffen. "Hurry!" he said.

At the next turning she glanced back and saw only a blank wall behind them.

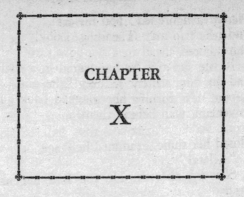

CHAPTER

X

As Dilvish edged along the northeast periphery of the room, the tableau became clearer—the upset brazier, the dark design, the groping tentacle, the half-stripped girl upon the barrow, the faintly glowing prints of cloven hoofs . . .

He sheathed his blade as quietly as he could, feeling that it would be of little use against the possessor of such a member. Better to have both hands free, he decided as he moved forward quickly to take hold of the barrow's handles. The tip of the tentacle found the wheel at about the same time. He raised the barrow and drew it back. The tentacle slipped away. There came a thrashing in the waters below. He continued to back off.

Suddenly, a tentacle shot up to twice his height above the lip of the pit. Dilvish veered sharply to his left as he backed away. The tentacle fell with a great slapping sound upon the place he would have occupied had he continued in a straight line. It began to toss wildly about. He was soon out of range, however, and near the opening of the eastern passageway. He turned the wheelbarrow and headed up it. The splashing noises continued behind him.

It was only as he hurried away that he really had an opportunity to look at the barrow's occupant. He drew in his breath sharply and halted, lowering the conveyance, moving around to its front. Arlata's chest still rose and fell slowly. He closed her tunic, examined her face.

"Arlata?"

She did not stir. He repeated her name in a louder voice. There was no reaction. He slapped her lightly. Her head rolled to the side and remained there.

He returned to the vehicle's rear and began pushing again. The first room he came to was a storeroom full of tools. He went on, inspecting several others. The fourth was a linen room, heaped with folded curtains, blankets, coverlets, rugs, towels. A flash of red came and went behind its solitary small window as he pushed Arlata in and unfastened her bonds. He transferred her then to a pile of linens and unfolded a blanket to cover her.

Closing the door behind him, he turned up the hallway and stared. It became better illuminated before his eyes, all of the brightness emanating from just a few small windows. And in this increased light he saw again the cloven hoofmarks. He began to follow them and continued until his path intersected a carpeted hallway, where they vanished. For a moment he stood undecided. Then, shrugging, he turned to the left. The way seemed long and straight and bright before him, but then a peculiar thing occurred. The air shimmered, then darkened, about six paces ahead of him. A smoky coalescence followed. Suddenly, he faced a stone wall.

He laughed.

"All right," he said.

He did an about-face, then headed up the remaining branch of the hallway, checking as he moved whether his blade was loose in its sheath.

Odil, Hodgson, and Derkon glutted themselves in the pantry they had located.

"What the hell is that?" Derkon asked, pointing with a leg of mutton at the small skylight which was suddenly a blazing, brilliant red.

The others looked, then looked away as the red faded and the brightening continued.

"Are we on fire?" Odil wondered; and it ceased then and the dimness followed.

"More general, I think," Hodgson replied.

"I don't understand," said Odil.

"Everything outside seems to be happening countless times faster than it normally does."

"And we did it somehow—when we broke the maintenance spell?"

"I'd say."

"I thought it would just knock down a wall, or something like that."

Derkon laughed.

"But it would probably kill us to leave the place now! Strand us in a wasteland, deliver us to monsters—or worse . . ."

Derkon laughed again, tossed him a bottle.

"Here. You need a drink. You're beginning to get the picture."

Odil unstopped it and downed a mouthful.

Then, "What are we to do?" he asked. "If we can't get out of here—"

"Exactly. What's the alternative? Do you recall our original intention?"

Odil, who had been raising the bottle for another swallow, lowered it, eyes widening.

"Go to that thing and try to bind it? Just the three of us? The shape we're in?"

Hodgson nodded.

"Unless we can bring Vane to his senses—or locate Dilvish—it's just the three of us."

"What good will it do us now, even if we succeed?"

Hodgson dropped his eyes. Derkon made a growling sound.

"Maybe none at all," Derkon said. "But the Old One is the only thing in sight with the sort of power that might be able to reverse what is going on—to take us back."

"How will we do it?"

Derkon shrugged and looked at Hodgson as if for advice. When it was not forthcoming, he said, "Well, I was thinking that a modification—and combination—of several of the strongest binding spells I know—"

"They're for demons, aren't they?" Odil inquired. "That thing is no demon."

"No, but the principle is the same for binding anything."

"True. But the normal Names of Power probably would not control in the case of an Old One. You'd have to go back to the Elder Gods for the necessary nomenclature."

Derkon slapped his thigh.

"Good! I've got you thinking about it!" he said. "You work out the proper list of Names while I figure the modifications. We'll put them together when we get there and tie the old boy in knots!"

Odil shook his head.

"It's not that easy . . ."

"Try!"

"I'll help," said Hodgson when Odil looked dubious. "I can think of no other plan."

They talked of it as they finished eating, and Derkon assembled the spell. Finally he said, "Why postpone it?" and the others nodded.

They departed the pantry and halted.

"We came this way," said Hodgson, frowning, placing his hand upon the wall to his right. "Didn't we?"

"I thought so," Derkon said, looking at Odil, who nodded.

"We did. However—" He turned to the left. "This is the only way now open to us."

They moved in that direction.

Hodgson cleared his throat.

"Something is obviously guiding us away from our objective," he said as they passed through a wide, low hall. "Either Jelerak is back and toying with us, or the Old One has become aware of our intentions and is steering us away. In which case—"

"No," said Derkon. "I am sufficiently sensitive to feel that something else is behind it."

"What?"

"I do not know, but it does not seem unkindly disposed toward us."

Leaving the hall and taking another turn, they came to a small alcove. Displayed upon a heavy wooden table within it were three blades of various lengths, each with a scabbard and belt.

"Something like that," he said. "I'll wager that each of us will find one of them suitable."

"As suitable as a blade can ever be," Odil remarked as they moved forward and took them up.

The dark thing burst forth upon the open rampart, eyes flashing beneath a pale, sooty, yellow sky. It tossed its head, looking upon a pulsing landscape of sand and stone. The winds screamed about it and were harsh.

I have come, it said in a special way, *to this place where we can talk. I will help you.*

Perhaps, came the reply from all around.

What do you mean, "Perhaps"?

The man thinks you a demon, little brother.

Let him. We've other problems.

True. So let us confine ourselves to the Hounds.

I do not understand.

All the more reason to pay heed.

Limping slightly as he approached the threshold to the main hall—each passage closed off behind him, no other way open to him—Baran saw Vane at the same moment Vane saw him. Baran hesitated. Vane did not.

Brandishing his blade, a curse upon his lips, Vane rushed forward.

When he had crossed half the distance between them, a ripping noise occurred beside Vane, and out of the dark V which had opened in the air to his left came forth an enormous hand. It seized him about the middle, raised him above the floor, then cast him, bouncing and sliding, across the hall, his rust-tipped weapon spinning free of his grip, to fetch him with a crash up against the mirrored wall, where he lay still.

The Hand hovered in midair as Baran stumped into the hall. Vane's head turned toward him and he moaned softly.

Slowly closing itself into a fist, the Hand moved toward Vane.

"That's Vane!"

"And there's Baran!"

"Get him!"

Baran's gaze flew to the rear of the hall, where

three figures had entered. He recognized the former prisoners, saw immediately that they were armed. They commenced sprinting in his direction, their images multiplied in the mirrors at either side.

Baran drew his blade as he turned toward them, but let it hang loosely at his right side. His left hand was still tucked firmly behind his belt.

The great Hand, poised to strike Vane, opened wide and fled through the air toward the approaching men. Seeing it come, Odil ducked, swung at it and missed. It struck Derkon, knocking him off his feet and into Hodgson, sending both men sprawling. The Hand immediately turned and flew after Odil, fingers crooked, thumb bending.

Odil was almost upon Baran, his blade upraised, when he was seized from behind in a massive grasp and lifted above the floor. Blood rushed from his nose and his ribs cracked audibly as he struck downward, cutting at one of the fingers.

Then, off to the right, Baran detected a flash of green. It was the new prisoner, the one Semirama had made such a fuss over . . .

The Hand jerked, tightening violently, and Odil emitted a brief, bubbling cry before going limp in its grasp, the blade slipping from his fingers. Then the Hand rushed forward, opening, and Odil's crushed form was hurled toward Dilvish.

Dilvish sidestepped and kept coming as the body flashed by him, landing with a thud somewhere to the rear. But now the Hand was rushing directly toward him.

Dilvish, who had seen Hodgson and Derkon regaining their feet and a slow movement from the fallen form of Vane across the hall, knew that none of these others would be able to help him at this point. He sought through his magical arsenal after some weapon even as he dove forward and rolled beneath the Hand. His green boots struck the floor and he was borne immediately to his feet, to whirl, blade raised, and strike the little finger from the rushing Hand.

The Hand convulsed. The finger, dripping a pale fluid which turned to smoke, struck the floor and rolled for half a turn.

Baran raised his blade and backed away. The Hand straightened, dropped, and swung in a floor-skimming slap at Dilvish.

Dilvish leaped over it and cut downward with his blade as it passed, nicking the back of the thumb. Derkon and Hodgson came up beside him as he landed.

"Spread out!" he said. "Hit it from all sides! Keep apart!"

The Hand halted in a backswing as three blades were raised against it from various angles. Dilvish rushed forward and cut at it. It swung at him and he leaped back. Even as it moved, Hodgson and Derkon were both upon it, cutting. It brushed them away and Dilvish darted in and nicked it again. Smoke now rose from half a dozen cuts upon it.

In the mirror, as he danced back, Dilvish saw that Vane was crawling slowly forward, his blade in his hand.

Derkon, recovered, fell upon the Hand again and Dilvish moved to do the same. At that moment, however, the Hand shot straight up into the air, out of their reach. Seeing that Baran intended to swat them one by one from above, Dilvish instantly raised his blade. The others did the same. It was then that Dilvish decided upon his magical weapon, and in a steady voice he began speaking the ancient words.

It was one of the lesser of the Awful Sayings, to lay absolute, impenetrable blackness upon a locale for an entire day. Dilvish heard a gasp from Derkon as that one overheard a phrase.

The Hand circled, feinted several times. Then a mournful sighing sound filled the hall, accompanied by an abrupt drop in temperature. As Dilvish finished speaking, the light began to roll away, as in a succession of waves.

They were left in total darkness.

"Get him!" Dilvish breathed, and he moved quickly.

Blade extended before him now, he headed toward the place where Baran had been standing. He heard a great swishing sound descending and threw himself flat. It passed.

He scrambled to his feet and continued on. He heard a sharp intake of breath nearby. But it was not repeated and he was not certain as to its direction. He heard a brief scuffle, and Derkon and Hodgson both cursed. They had apparently run into one another.

There came another swishing and a thud from somewhere behind him as the Hand slapped the floor.

It seemed that Baran could have moved to his left, his right or backward. But going backward would most readily have led him into a corner. Left seemed to offer the greatest degree of freedom, so Dilvish turned, moved again, blade waving before him.

He would have sworn that a tiny bit of light reached him from the direction of the sitting room. But that was impossible. The Awful Saying would have dampened every light source.

It grew brighter.

Vague outlines were now becoming perceptible. Something was wrong. He knew of no power which would break an Awful Saying. Yet a faint illumination was definitely creeping into the hall.

High overhead, the Hand groped ghostlike through the middle air. A few moments more, and it could be dropping toward him again. He cast his eyes wildly about. There was movement. The forms of crouched men. But which one?

Suddenly there came the sounds of another scuffle, but this one ended in a brief scream. Then it resumed. It came from ahead and somewhat to the right. Yes! There!

Two figures writhed together upon the floor. There came another cry even as Dilvish began his cautious advance.

The darkness continued to ebb. Something overhead caught his eyes. The Hand, now plainly visible, clutched and opened, began to twitch spasmodically. It dipped and hovered again several times.

Then he saw below. The huge form of Baran lay atop that of Vane, the edge of Vane's blunted blade halfway into the neck. Neither figure stirred, but now the Hand was dipping again.

Fingers extended, it reached beneath the upper, stilled form. Trembling then, it lifted Baran into the air. Beneath it, Dilvish could see where Baran's blade protruded from Vane's breast.

Shaking steadily, the Hand rose higher in the increasing light. The black V behind it stood out clearly against the lesser darkness. Then the Hand began to retreat into that aperture, taking Baran with it.

Dilvish and the others watched the slow withdrawal until only three massive fingertips were visible. Then these, too, slid out of sight and the rift closed with a sound like a thunderclap.

Immediately, they became aware of movement all about them.

Turning, Dilvish saw a series of gigantic faces within the mirrors which lined the walls—black, red, yellow, pale; some almost human, many far removed from any resemblance to mankind; some amused, several placid, others frowning; all, bathed in a supernatural light, their gazes too mighty to return. He looked away, and in that moment they vanished and the yellow light returned to the hall at its fullest strength.

He shook himself and rubbed his eyes, wondering whether the others had seen what he thought he had.

"There was a couch in that little room," he heard Hodgson saying to Derkon.

"Yes."

He sheathed his blade and followed them as they bore Vane's body out of the hall. While they arranged it upon the couch, he tore down a hanging, took it back, and cast it over Odil's remains. Then he moved toward the rear of the hall.

"Dilvish. Wait."

He halted, and shortly the other two came up beside him.

"Are we together?" Derkon asked him.

"Physically, for the moment," Dilvish said. "But I still have my own business to take care of, and it's likely to prove even nastier than this was."

"Oh," said Derkon. Then, "How do you propose getting away afterward?" he asked.

Dilvish shook his head.

"I've no idea," he replied. "Maybe I won't be able to."

"That seems an awfully defeatist—"

The floor began to vibrate. The walls seemed to sway, and a mighty groaning sound rose up out of the bowels of the castle. Phantom forms fled briefly across the room, passing through mirror or wall. The light grew more stable. Derkon clutched Hodgson's shoulder for support as the castle gave a final shudder before settling down.

Then a silence came over the place, shortly to be tapped—very lightly—by the ticking of the great clock.

"Always something doing around here, isn't there?" Derkon remarked, grinning weakly.

The big doors at the end of the hall rattled, as with a heavy gust of wind. Dilvish turned slowly in that direction, as if hypnotized.

"I wonder," he said, "whether it has stopped."

He began walking back. After a moment's hesitation the others followed him.

Partway across the hall, they heard a crash followed by a rumbling sound from outside. It grew louder, as if approaching, then ceased abruptly. The door rattled again.

Dilvish continued on, passing the clock, entering the sitting room without a glance at the form on the couch, crossing to the door, and gripping its handle.

"You're going outside?" Hodgson asked.

"I want to see."

Dilvish opened the door and a chill breeze crept in past them. They appeared to be situated in the midst of a great, pale plain, ringed by a range of misty, coppery mountains which faded off into a twilit sky. It took several moments for them to realize that the shrunken, straw-colored disk about halfway to midheaven must, as the major source of illumination, be the remains of the sun. Stars were plainly visible up to three of its own diameters about it. A shower of meteors suddenly cut the prospect above the mountains to the left. A yellow dust cloud drifted and settled, rose again, swirled, vanished. Hodgson coughed. The air had a raw, metallic flavor to it.

Suddenly a pair of gigantic rocks appeared upon the plain, bounced along it for a time, fell still. It took the rumbling noise perhaps half a minute to reach them. Before that occurred, however, a huge red hand came down out of the sky and scooped them up, shaking them like thunder above the watchers' heads.

Dilvish followed the ruddy arm with his eyes up into the misty area, where, after several moments' staring, he was able to discern the outline of a colossal kneeling body, vaguely human in form, stars shining through it, meteors in its hair. It raised the arm an unimaginable distance into the sky, fist shaking. It was only then that the cube-like shape of the rocks registered itself upon Dilvish's understanding.

He looked away. His eyes, now accommodated to the scale of things and the wavelengths involved, had less difficulty in discerning other monolithic beings—like the great black figure, head propped on one hand, two arms folded across its breast, the fingers of a fourth hand stroking the south-eastern mountaintops above which it reclined; the shadowy white figure with one eye and one gaping socket, which leaned upon a staff that reached higher than the sun, stars like fireflies caught in its floppy hat; the slow-dancing woman with many breasts; the jackal-headed one; the whirling tower of fire . . .

Dilvish looked at his companions, saw that they were staring, too, expressions of unutterable awe upon their faces.

The dice were rolled again and the dust rose about them. The celestial figures leaned forward. The black one grinned and moved one of his hands to take up the cubes. The red one straightened and withdrew. Dilvish closed the door.

"The Elder Gods . . ." Hodgson said. "I never thought I'd be permitted to look upon them . . ."

"For what," said Derkon, with as much caution as awe, "do you think they might be gaming?"

"Not being privy to the councils of the gods," Dilvish replied, "I can't say for certain. But I've a feeling I had better conclude my business as quickly as possible."

The rumbling sound reached them and the big doors inside rattled again.

"Gentlemen, excuse me," Dilvish said, and he turned and departed the room.

Hodgson and Derkon regarded one another for only a moment, then hurried after.

"You will be accompanying me?" Dilvish asked as they drew up alongside him.

"Despite the dangers you mentioned, I feel that we may all ultimately be safer by staying together," Derkon answered.

"I agree," said Hodgson. "But would you mind telling us where it is that we are headed?"

"I do not know," Dilvish answered, "but I am coming to trust the genius of this place, whatever it may be, and I am willing to surrender myself to its guidance again. Our objectives may be the same."

"What if it is Jelerak, leading you on to some doom?"

Dilvish shook his head.

"Jelerak, I am certain, wouldn't have halted the show to feed me the decent meal I received on the way over here."

They entered the rear passageway Dilvish had taken earlier on his flight from the lower regions. The door still creaked, but the corridor was only about a fourth its former length. There was no right turn at its end, and there were no slave quarters to the left. The room of the blue flame had vanished completely. The walls were all paneled in dark wood and the windows rectangular affairs that slid up and down, set in wooden frames, possessed of peculiar shading devices, draped with white lace curtains. They mounted a wooden stair. There were more paintings on the walls in that peculiar, bright, suggestive style Dilvish had noted earlier.

Outside, they heard again the rumble of the dice, followed this time by something like titanic peals of laughter.

Another turn, and they entered one of the galleries, narrower now and with a long carpet down its center. The windows had grown more rectangular here also, though the walls and floors remained stone.

"Do you feel that this place is growing smaller even as we move about in it?" Hodgson asked.

"Yes," Dilvish replied, looking back. "It seems to be turning itself into something else. And have you noticed that there have been no options, no choices, as to the way we are to go? It is being very definite now."

Ahead, Dilvish heard a series of strange chirping sounds. Abruptly, he halted. Hodgson and Derkon did the same, raising their hands and moving them about. Something was barring the way.

The air began to shimmer before them. It grew opaque, darkened further. Dilvish found himself touching a stone wall.

He turned away. The air was shimmering about six paces behind him. He moved toward it, along with the others. The phenomenon was repeated. The window provided illumination within their sudden cell, but a quick inspection revealed that there was no way to get from it to one of the other windows along the smooth outer wall.

"You were saying," Derkon observed, "that you trust the genius of this place."

Dilvish snarled.

"There is a reason. There must be a reason!" he snapped.

"Timing," said Hodgson. "I think it's timing. We're too early."

"For what?" Derkon asked.

"We'll find out when that wall goes away."

"You really think it will?"

"Of course. The front wall is sufficient to stop us from going ahead. The rear one is to stop us from going away from here."

"An interesting notion."

"So I would suggest we face the front wall and be ready for anything."

"There may be something to what you say," Dilvish stated, positioning himself and taking his blade into his hand.

They heard the dice of the gods again, and the laughter. But this time the laughter went on and on, growing louder until it rocked the walls of the place, until it seemed to be coming from directly overhead.

The wall began to shimmer and fade at the same moment that a groaning, cracking sound began somewhere beyond it. A quick glance showed Dilvish that the rear wall was not departing.

As soon as the way was clear they moved ahead. But they halted after only a few paces, frozen by the sight in the chamber before them.

Countless rubbery tentacles upon the rim of the pit supported the thing which had drawn itself partway up. At the northeastern edge of the hole stood the man Dilvish had first known as Weleand, a band of ruddy glass across his eyes. At his rear stood Semirama, perfectly still, as both of them regarded the risen form of Tualua. Overhead, the roof had been split open, and even as Dilvish and his companions watched, a set of gigantic fingers entered, curved, took hold of a section of roof, crumpled it in a single motion and drew it aside. Great timbers fell and the starry sky was suddenly visible. Towering there was the enormous figure of a many-breasted woman, an unnatural light emanating from her form. She reached again, down through the opening she had made, and delicately, almost tenderly, took hold of the grotesque figure crouched upon the pit and raised it, moving it carefully through the jagged opening and upward.

"No!" Jelerak cried, pushing the goggles down to hang about his neck and glaring upward, eyes dancing. "No! Give him back! I need him!"

The sorcerer raced about the pit to where one of the fallen beams reached from the floor up to the overhead opening. He seized hold of it and began to climb.

"Return him, I say!" he cried. "No one steals from Jelerak! Not even a goddess!"

Halting halfway up the beam, he drew the red wand and pointed it.

"I said stop! Bring him back!"

The hand continued its slow withdrawal. Jelerak made a gesture and white fire fled from the tip of the wand, bathing the back of the hand in the sky.

"He *is* Jelerak!" said Dilvish, galvanized to action, sprinting forward.

The hand had halted and Jelerak was climbing again, nearing the broken roof.

Dilvish reached the edge of the pit, raced about its edge.

"Come back yourself, you bastard!" he cried. "I've got something for you!"

Now a second great hand had come into view above the mounting form, descending.

"I demand that you heed me!" Jelerak shouted, and then he saw the fingers opening, reaching.

He raised the wand and the hand was bathed in white light. The wand had no other apparent effect and was shortly knocked from his grasp as he was seized and himself raised, still remonstrating, into the twilit sky.

"He's mine!" Dilvish cried when he reached the foot of the beam. "I've followed too long to relinquish him here! Return him!"

But the hands were already out of sight and the figure had turned away.

Dilvish stretched as if to climb the beam himself, when he felt a hand upon his arm.

"You can't reach him by going his way," Semirama said. "Which did you want, justice or revenge?"

"Both!" Dilvish cried.

"Then at least half your wish is granted. He is in the hands of the Elder Gods."

"It isn't fair!" Dilvish said through clenched teeth.

"Fair?" She laughed. "You talk to me of fairness—I, who have just found the form of my ancient love when Jelerak's death or the breaking of his will is about to end my existence?"

Dilvish turned and looked at her, saw past her. From high above came a great roll of laughter, receding.

Black and Arlata had just entered the chamber. Dilvish took hold of Semirama's hand and sank slowly to his knees. He heard a clatter of hoofs.

"Dilvish, what is it?" came Black's voice. "Our entrance to this chamber was barred until but a moment ago."

Dilvish looked at him, released Semirama's hand, gestured toward the roof.

"He's gone. Weleand was Jelerak—but the Elder Gods have taken him."

Black snorted.

"I knew who he was. I almost had him here earlier, in my human form."

"Your what?"

"The spell I've been working on since the Garden of Blood—I used it to free myself from the statue form. I was still conscious after Jelerak had frozen me to stone to free Arlata." He nodded toward the girl who was just now approaching, then went on. "I recognized him as Jelerak the moment that he did it. When I was free, I continued this way. I found her and her horse and freed them. I had to lay a spell upon her to get her out of the way. I left her in a cave down the hillside with certain protections upon it. Then—"

"Dilvish, who is this underdeveloped child?" Semirama asked.

Dilvish rose to his feet as Arlata hastily repaired her rent tunic.

"Queen Semirama of Jandar," he began, "this is the Lady Arlata of Marinta, whom I encountered on my journey to this place. She bears a striking resemblance to one I once knew well, long ago . . ."

"The irony is hardly lost on me," Semirama said, smiling and extending her hand, palm downward. "My child, I—"

Her smile vanished and she jerked her hand back, covering it with the other.

"No . . ." She turned away. "No!"

She raised her hands to cover her face and began running toward the eastern corridor.

"What did I do?" asked Arlata. "I do not understand . . ."

"Nothing," Dilvish told her. "Nothing. Wait here!"

He began running toward the corridor along which he had earlier pushed Arlata in the barrow. When he reached it, he discovered that it had become a bare alcove with white plastered walls, a wooden stair leading down to the right. He descended quickly.

The others saw a shadow pass overhead, a great black arm descending. Derkon rushed into the north gallery to peer out of the nearest window. Hodgson followed him, as did Arlata moments later. Black lowered his head, studying the fallen roofing material.

Staring out the window, they saw the massive black hand moving slowly, very slowly, toward one of the farther walls. It seemed almost to halt before it made contact, yet they felt the vibration all around them and the entire castle chimed—a single note—like a huge crystal bell.

The heavens began to dance and the ground shifted slightly. Looking up, they saw the smiling face of the dark one, fading, fading, gone.

The sun plunged into the west.

"Gods!" Derkon cried. "It's starting again!"

Nearby, to their right, the air began to shimmer and condense.

Dilvish tore down the steps and, turning, rubbed his eyes, disoriented. A small archway at the foot of the stair led into the rear of the main hall, at the place where the creaking door of the back corridor had been. He passed through quickly and saw the collapsed form of Semirama near the center of the room.

As he rushed toward her, her form seemed to alter, shrinking, becoming more angular. Her hair had turned pure white. Her revealing garments now showed parchmentlike skin and the outlines of bones.

But even as he drew near, a certain lightening of the air above her caused him to slow. For a moment he felt the awful presence of the thing he had seen hovering above the pit before the hand out of the heavens had snatched it away. There even seemed a vague outline of the Old One, tentacles extended, reaching toward her. Yet there was nothing of menace to the gesture. Entirely the contrary. It was as if the creature were reaching out to soothe, to grant some unnatural grace. A moment only the vision persisted, barely beyond the point that might mark it as an aberration of the lighting, an affliction of the retina. Then it was gone, and the tiny form upon the floor turned to dust before him.

When he reached the spot, there was very little to see. Even the garments had decomposed in wispy outline near his feet. Only—

A movement to his left caught his attention.

The mirror . . .

The mirror no longer reflected the main hall as it lay about him. Instead of the other mirror upon the opposite wall, it now showed a wide, curved, white stone staircase up which the figures were slowly moving. The woman was undoubtedly Semirama, as he had known her before death's recent interruption. And the man . . .

Although there was something familiar about the man, it was not until he turned his head and their eyes met that Dilvish saw that they could have been brothers. The other was somewhat larger than himself and possibly a bit older, but their features were almost identical. A slight smile came to the other's lips.

"Selar . . ." Dilvish whispered.

And then a sound like the chiming of a great crystal bell filled the air. Cracks ran like black lightning across the mirror, and pieces of it began to fall away as the entire castle shuddered and jerked.

Dilvish's last view of the pair on the stairway was of their unconcerned ascent and passage among dark blue curtains hung at the rear wall above, and disappearing behind them, before that section of glass also slipped away. Semirama, holding to the other's right arm, never looked back.

Dilvish dropped to one knee, to reach amid the dust before him. He raised a chain from which a small locket depended. He slipped it into his pocket.

CHAPTER

XI

"THIS way!" Black called. "Hurry! We are moving faster than before!"

Hodgson, Derkon, and Arlata came back into the chamber.

"What is it, Dark One?" Derkon asked.

"You come here," Black answered. "I've something for you."

Derkon obeyed.

"There." Black pointed with a cloven hoof at a streak of red among the rubble. "Pick it up."

Derkon stopped and retrieved it.

"Jelerak's wand?" he asked.

"The Red Wand of Falkyntyne. Bring it along. Hurry!"

Black turned away and moved toward the alcove through which Dilvish had departed. The others followed him.

"Dark One," said Derkon, "I follow. But what is happening? Why are we running?"

"This room still exists only because we are in

it. We are helping the house to get rid of an extra wing by departing . . ."

"House?"

"It has decided upon a smaller scale this time around. But the main reason is that the Great Flash will soon occur, for we left at a very fast pace, as the house requested—"

"Excuse me, Dark One," Hodgson shouted as they passed through the alcove and started down upon the stair, "but this Great Flash—are you referring to . . . ?"

"The creation of the universe," Black finished. "Yes. We are going all the way around. At any rate, after the flash we will be passing through a dangerous belt inhabited by beings which would do us the worst sort of harm. The house may be able to keep many of them out, but a few—"

Black reached the bottom of the stair and the flash occurred.

All color fled, and the world was black and white, light and darkness. Hodgson saw through the flesh of the girl before him—dark skeleton within a bright integument—and of Derkon before her, to a sort of flickering soul-light, beautiful among the dark geometry through which they passed, to Black—who was a pure and glorious sheet of flame—sweeping across the floor to where another burned within a mortal prison—

"The angles!" he heard Black say. "They will most likely come in at the corners of the hall! Use not the points of your weapons, for these will be powerless! Strike with the curve of your blade, and use a curving cut—save for you, Derkon! You must use the wand!"

"Against what? How?" Derkon cried as something of color and normal form returned to the hall about them and he sighted Dilvish standing at its center, ahead, blade drawn.

"The Hounds of Thandolos! The Red Wand has its greatest power in the hands of a black adept. There is nothing subtle about it. It is one of the most efficient magical blasting instruments ever created. Its operation is purely a function of the will, and it draws upon its wielder's life forces. Yours should be high and blazing now, having just passed through the Creation Flame! Let us stay together at the hall's center—in a circle!"

The lighting had returned to what passed as normal in this place before they reached Dilvish, the chandelier still blazing as high as before. The broken body of the demon had vanished. The hall seemed smaller with the mirrors all in shards, the walls blank and gray. From its place near the front, the tall clock hummed, its dial a shimmering blur.

Hodgson began muttering as something shadowy stirred in the corner nearest the clock.

"The gods you invoke have not yet been born," Black stated.

The figure which emerged was as sharp and angular and unrecallable as a burst of static electricity. It was dark and it stood upright, and there was a vaguely lupine air about it as it sprang forward —also something cold and partaking of a primal hunger which nothing in the new universe might fully satisfy.

"Use the wand! Blast it!" said Black.

"I can't make it work!" said Derkon, the red rod raised before him, lines of tightness about his eyes and mouth.

Dilvish swung his blade in an arc before the advancing creature, repeating the gesture rapidly, over and over again. It darted toward him, halted, drew back. The air was filled with the sound of heavy breathing. Back in the corner from which it had emerged, another creature jerked forth, this one dropping to all fours and darting wide past the confrontation of its fellow and the arcing blade. Arlata scratched a curved line upon the floor before it and struck an en garde position, the point of her weapon moving constantly. It scurried to flank her, and Hodgson scratched a continuation of the curve and began waving his blade before him also. Another of the creatures was coming out of the same corner, and turning his head, Black saw that they were now appearing in all corners of the hall, including those overhead.

More and more of them approached, crowding nearer and nearer, darting, retreating, heads snaking forward, snapping back. Dilvish was pressed on three sides. Derkon uttered imprecations as he shook the wand and waved it.

Then Black snorted and reared. Fires danced in his eyes as he advanced to break the circle and fall upon the Hounds besetting Dilvish. Great gouts of fire spewed from his nostrils upon the angular, darting forms. One fell to the floor and began thrashing about. Another fled. The third sprang upon his back. He reared again and Dilvish's blade slashed across the creature atop him. It howled and slipped to the floor as two more sprang at him.

Dilvish cut at another and Black struck forward and breathed more flames. Five more leaped at them as this occurred.

Abruptly, a great flash of light appeared and Hounds were falling away everywhere.

"I've got it!" Derkon announced, the Red Wand blazing like a star in his hand. "It was almost too simple!"

He directed it first upon those Hounds nearest them, blasting them back across the hall. Some slithered into corners and vanished. Others lay smoldering, jerking, changing shape. Those which had been approaching—sliding down walls, bounding across the floor—halted, milled, transformed themselves into hissing packs. The hall was filled with the sounds of their breathing.

Immediately, Derkon turned the wand upon the nearest pack, shattering and scattering it. The others howled and raced forward.

Dilvish and Black hurried to rejoin the circle as Derkon continued to wield the wand against the oncoming creatures. By then, Derkon was beginning to breathe heavily himself.

Hodgson struck at one of the beasts which had gotten by. It hissed, withdrew, and came at him again. Dilvish cut at another, Arlata at a third and a fourth. Black scraped arcs upon the floor with his metal hoofs and breathed fire above them. Derkon swung the wand again.

"They're falling back!" Hodgson gasped as Derkon continued to swing the wand in widening arcs, his face a mixture of pain and exultation.

The Hounds were retreating. It seemed that wherever there was an angle, one was sliding into it and out of existence. Laughing, Derkon hurled bolt after bolt at them, blasting them along their way. Dilvish straightened. Hodgson massaged his arm. Arlata smiled faintly.

No one spoke again until all of them had departed. And they remained together for a long while, back to back, watching the corners, running their gazes over angles.

Finally, Derkon lowered the wand, lowered his head, and rubbed his eyes.

"Takes a lot out of you," he said softly.

Hodgson clasped his shoulder.

"Well done," he said.

Arlata clasped his hand. Dilvish came over and repeated the gesture.

"They have all departed," Black announced, "and are fleeing back to their own regions. Our velocity is mounting enormously."

"I could use some wine," Derkon said.

"Anticipated," said Black. "Apply to the cabinet across the way."

Derkon raised his head. Dilvish turned his.

The once-gray walls were now white and of a plastered appearance. A group of paintings hung upon the one to the left, a small red and yellow tapestry depicting a boar hunt upon the right-hand one. Directly below the tapestry was a mahogany cabinet. There were bottles of wine and other beverages within, some of them entirely strange. Black indicated one of these latter, a squarish bottle containing an amber fluid.

"Just the thing for my sort," he said to Dilvish. "Pour some of that into yon silver bowl."

Dilvish uncorked it and sniffed.

"Smells like something you'd use in a lamp," he observed. "What is it?"

"It is closely related to demonjuice and other items in my natural fare. Pour out a lot."

Later, Arlata studied Dilvish over her wineglass.

"You alone appear to have achieved your goal," she said, "after a fashion."

"Yes," he replied. "The weight of many years has been lifted. Yet—It is not the way that I had thought it would be. I don't know . . ."

"Yet you have succeeded," she said. "You have seen your enemy removed from the world. As for Tualua—I suppose that the poor creature is better off with the gods themselves, who count it as kin."

"I begrudge nothing its salvation," Dilvish said.

"And I am just beginning to realize how tired I am. Perhaps that is good. You—You will find other ways to better the world, I am certain, than with the use of a mighty slave."

She smiled.

"I'd like to think so," she said, "providing we ever find our way back to our world."

"Go back . . ." Dilvish said, as if the thought had occurred to him for the first time. "Yes. It might be good at that . . ."

"What will you do?"

He stared at her.

"I don't know," he answered. "I hadn't given it any thought."

"Over here!" Hodgson called out from around a corner where he had wandered with Derkon. "Come see!"

Dilvish downed his drink and left the glass atop the cabinet. Arlata placed hers beside it. The only urgency in the cry had been that of excitement. They walked toward the room in which the two sorcerers stood before a bay window. The room had not been present earlier.

The brightness beyond the window seemed to be increasing. When they came up beside the others and looked out, they saw a rapidly fluctuating landscape not without considerable patches of green beneath a sky traversed by a great, glowing golden arch.

"The sunbow is bright," said Derkon, "and you can just barely detect a light-dark pattern if you stare for a time. It may be a sign that we are slowing."

"I believe that you are right," said Dilvish after a while.

Hodgson turned away from the window, gestured widely.

"The entire place has changed," he said. "I am going to have a look around."

"I," said Dilvish, "am not," and he returned to the bar.

The others followed Hodgson, save for Black, who raised his muzzle and turned his head.

"A little more of the substitute demonjuice, if you please," he said.

Dilvish refilled the bowl and poured himself another glass of wine.

Black took another drink, then looked at Dilvish.

"I promised to help you," he said slowly, "until Jelerak had been disposed of."

"I know," Dilvish replied.

"And what now, eh? What now?"

"I don't know."

"A number of alternatives present themselves to me."

"Such as . . . ?"

"Not important, not important. Only the one I choose is important."

"And what have you chosen?"

"It's been an interesting career so far. It would be a shame to end it at this point. I'm curious what will become of you, now that the big driving force in your life has been removed."

". . . and the rest of our arrangement?"

From no apparent source, a piece of folded parchment sealed with red wax and imprinted with a cloven hoofmark fell upon the floor between them. Black leaned forward and breathed upon it. It burst into flames.

"I have just scrapped our pact. Forget it."

Dilvish's eyes widened.

"You meet the damndest people in Hell," he said. "I sometimes doubt you really are a demon."

"I never said that I was."

"What, then?"

Black laughed.

"You may never know how close you came to finding out. Pour me the rest of that stuff. Then we'll go and get the lady's horse."

"Arlata's Stormbird?"

"Yes. A part of the hillside has accompanied us, so the cave should still be here. Jelerak was able to go out to it and bring her in. We might as well do the same and save the horse . . . Thank you."

Black lowered his head to drink again. Across the way, the clock made peculiar noises, beginning to slow.

Not reflecting anything within the room, a form took shape within the great iron-rimmed mirror. Holrun stared out, examining the small chamber, satisfied himself that it was empty and stepped forth.

He wore a soft, sleeveless leather jacket over a dusky knit shirt with palely embroidered cuffs; his trousers were a dark green sateen, bloused into wide-topped black boots; his *kellen*-hide belt was studded and bore a short, silver-chased scabbard at his right hip.

As he crossed the room, he heard voices from outside and moved to take up a position beside the door.

"It *has* become a lot smaller," he heard a masculine voice say.

"Yes, everything is changed," answered another.

"I rather like it this way," said the first.

"I wish we could find something worth plundering, though—for our troubles."

"I'll be happy just to get out of here," said a female voice. "I still have a dotted line."

"No problem there," said the second masculine voice, "as soon as it stops. Soon, I'd say."

"Yes, but where?"

"Wherever. Just to be alive in the world again will be good."

"Unless it stops on a desert, a glacier, or a sea bottom."

"I've a feeling," came the girl's voice, "that it knows where it is going and is changing to accommodate itself to the locale."

"Then," came the first masculine voice, "I've a feeling I'll like the place."

Holrun pushed open the door and stepped out into the corridor, where he immediately faced two drawn blades and a red wand.

"I take it you people are not interested in going home, then?" he said, raising his hands. "Point that wand somewhere else, huh?" he added. "I think I recognize it."

"You're Holrun," Derkon said, lowering the wand, "a member of the Council."

"Ex-member," Holrun corrected. "Where's the boss?"

"You mean Jelerak?" Hodgson asked. "Dead, I think. In the hands of the Elder Gods."

Holrun made a clicking noise with his tongue, looked up and down the hall.

"You call this place a castle? Doesn't look like any castle to me. What have you been doing to it?"

"How did you get here?" Derkon asked.

"The mirror. I'm the last one around who appreciates it. Are you three all that's left in the place?"

"There were others about—servants and such," Hodgson said, "but they all seem to have disappeared. We've explored most of the place and found no one else. There's only ourselves and Dilvish and Black—"

"Dilvish *is* here?"

"Yes. We left him downstairs."

"Come on. Show me the way."

Blades were sheathed and they led him to the stair.

Partway down, they felt a strong draft. When they reached the ground floor, they noted that the former double doors had become a single large one, and this stood open. It was night outside and the movements of the stars had slowed. When the sun came up, it swam rapidly but did not race into the heavens. It seemed to be slowing even as they watched. Before it reached the middle of the sky, the house gave a jolt and the sun stood still.

"We're here," Hodgson said, "wherever here is," and he looked out across a very green landscape toward the misty mountains. "Not bad," he remarked.

"If you have a thing for vegetation," Holrun said, as he stepped over the threshold and looked about.

Dilvish and Black were approaching, leading a white horse.

"Stormbird!" Arlata cried, racing forward to embrace the horse.

Dilvish smiled and passed her the reins.

"Gods!" Holrun said. "You want me to take a horse through into my sanctum?"

Arlata turned, eyes flashing.

"We go together or we do not go."

"It had better be well behaved," Holrun said, turning back toward the house. "Come on."

"I'm not going," Hodgson stated.

"What?" said Derkon. "You're joking!"

"No. I like it here."

"You don't know anything about the place."

"I like its looks—its feeling. If it disappoints me, I can always try the mirror."

"Wouldn't you know, the only white magician I ever liked . . . Well, good luck to you."

He extended his hand.

"Will anybody who *does* want to leave please come with me?" said Holrun. "I've got a lot of work ahead of me today."

They filed back into the house, Black's step slightly less sure-footed than usual.

Holrun dropped back as the others returned to the stair.

"So you're Dilvish?" he asked.

"That's right."

"You're not as heroic-looking as I thought you'd be. Say, do you recognize that wand Derkon is carrying?"

"It is the Red Wand of Falkyntyne."

"Does he know it?"

"Yes."

"Damn!"

"Why 'damn'?"

"I want it."

"Maybe you can make a deal with him."

"Maybe so. You really saw Jelerak get his?"

"Afraid so."

Holrun shook his head.

"I've got to have the whole story as soon as we get back so I can tell the Council. I may even join them again, now that their half-assed policy doesn't matter."

They mounted the stair, came to the room of the mirror, and entered. Holrun led them to the glass, activated its spell.

"Goodbye," Hodgson said.

"Good luck," Dilvish told him.

Holrun stepped into the mirror. Arlata nodded and smiled at Hodgson, then she and Dilvish led Stormbird into the glass, Derkon and Black following.

Then came a momentary rippling of reality, a feeling of intense cold. They emerged in Holrun's chamber.

"Out!" Holrun said immediately. "Get that horse out into the hall! All I need's some neat little brown piles on my pentagrams. Out! Out! You—Derkon!—wait a minute! I've been looking at that wand. I'd like it for my collection. What say I trade you one of the Green Wands of Omalskyne, the Mask of Confusion, and a sack of Frilian dream-dust for it?"

Derkon turned and looked at the objects Holrun was snatching from shelves.

"Ah, I don't know . . ." Derkon began.

Black leaned forward.

"That green wand is a fake," he said to Holrun.

"What do you mean? It works. I paid a bundle for it. Here, I'll show you—"

"I saw the originals destroyed at Sanglasso a thousand years ago."

Holrun lowered the wand, with which he had just begun tracing fiery diagrams in the air.

"A very good fake," Black added. "But I can show you how to test it."

"Damn!" Holrun said. "Wait till I catch that guy. He told me—"

"That Muri power-belt hanging on the wall is a phony, too."

"I've suspected that. Say, could I offer you a job?"

"It depends on how long we'll be here. If there is no place for the horse . . ."

"We'll find a place! We'll find one! I've always been very fond of horses . . ."

Outside, in the faintly glowing corridor, Arlata regarded Dilvish.

"I'm tired," she said.

He nodded.

"Me, too. What will you be doing after you've rested?"

"Going home," she said. "And yourself?"

He shook his head.

"It's been a long while since you've visited Elfland, hasn't it?"

He smiled as the others emerged from the chamber.

"Come on," Holrun said. "This way. I need a hot soak. And food. And music."

"It has been," Dilvish said as they followed him up the tunnel, "too long. Far too long."

Behind them, Black snorted something none of them recognized as a tune. The light grew before them. About them, the walls sparkled. Somewhere in the world the black doves were singing as they headed for their landing and their rest.

'ABOUT THE AUTHOR

ROGER ZELAZNY was born in Ohio, began writing at age twelve, holds degrees from Western Reserve and Columbia, has been a professional writer since 1962, is married, and lives in New Mexico with his wife Judy, sons Devin and Trent, and daughter Shannon. He is the author of nineteen novels and four story collections. He is a three-time winner of the Science Fiction Achievement Award ("Hugo"), has received the Science Fiction Writers of America Nebula Award on three occasions, the French Prix Apollo once, and has had one book chosen by the American Library Association as a Best Book for Young Adults. His works have been translated into twelve foreign languages and have been dramatized on stage, screen, and radio.

Roger worked for seven years as a federal civil servant before quitting to write full-time. He is a past secretary-treasurer of the Science Fiction Writers of America. His best-known books are probably *Lord of Light, Doorways in the Sand,* and his five-volume Amber series. He speaks often to campus audiences.